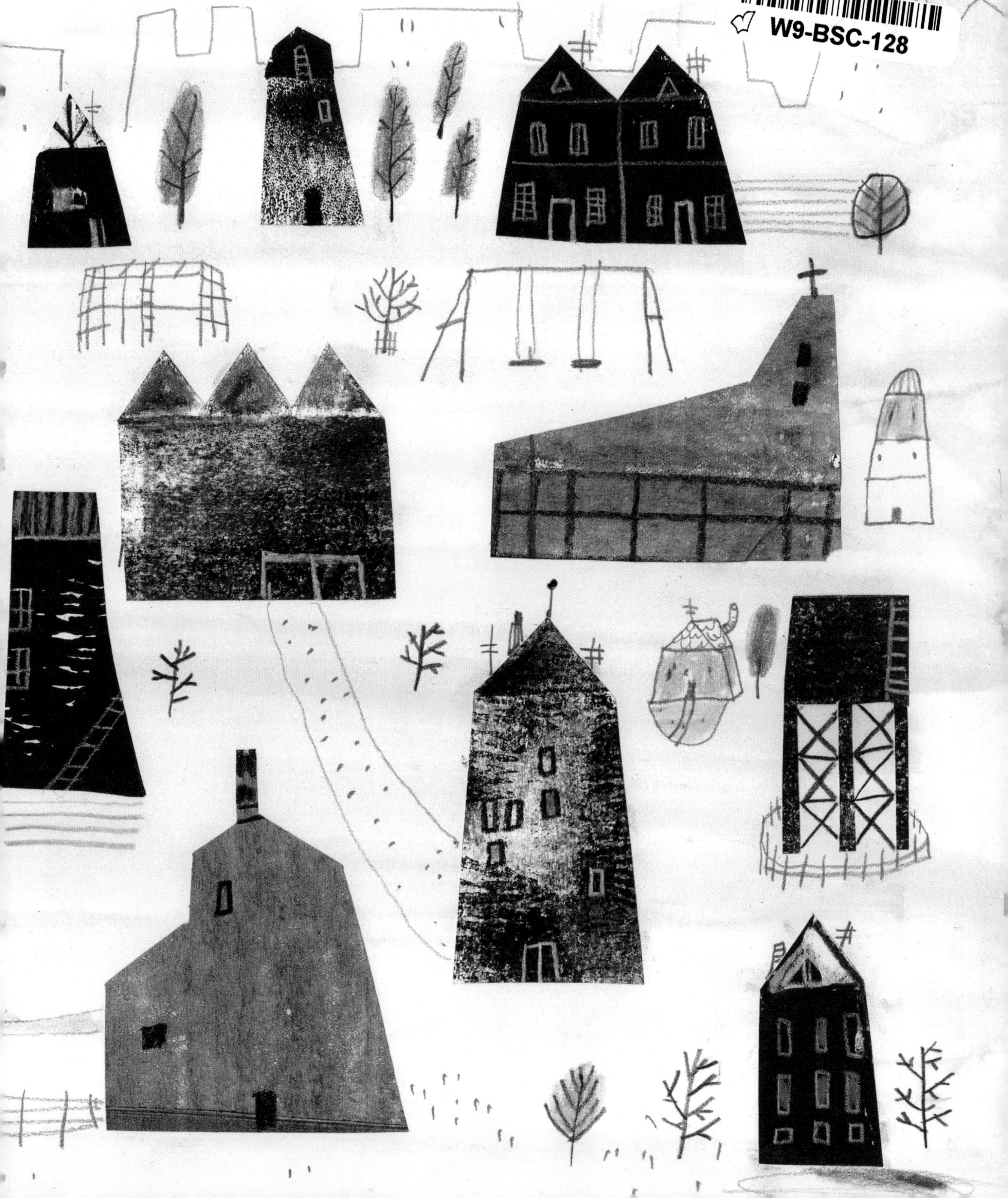

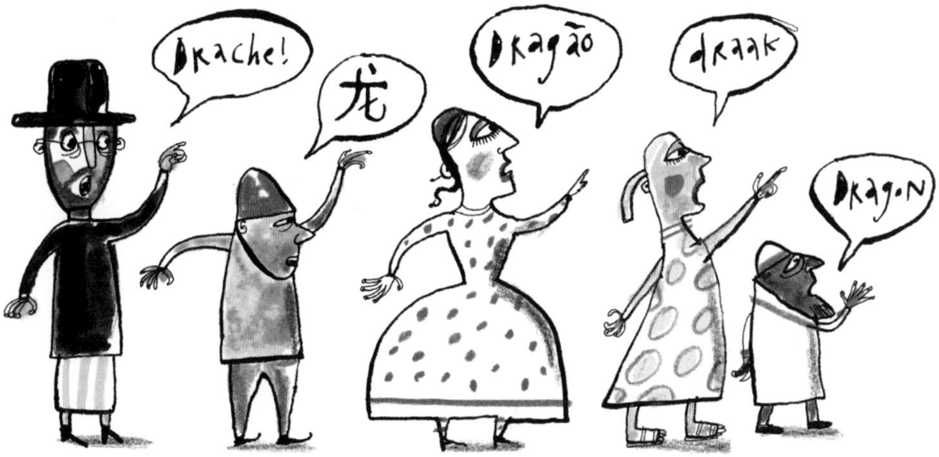
Drache!
龙
Dragão
draak
Dragon

Pic
J
Lawson
Main

For Ashey, our inquisitive word magician —
Daddy, Mommy, Sophie and JoJo always listen to
you spellbound.

JABL

To Frik Viljoen, Hendrik Odendaal, David Hunter
and Lourens and Jan Bosman.
For their belief in the power of stories and
communication and for their
longstanding friendship.

PG

YOUTH SERVICES
Falmouth Public Library
300 Main Street
Falmouth, MA 02540
508-457-2555

Text copyright © 2019 by JonArno Lawson
Illustrations copyright © 2019 by Piet Grobler
Published in Canada and the USA in 2019 by Groundwood Books

All rights reserved. No part of this publication may be reproduced,
stored in a retrieval system or transmitted, in any form or by any means,
without the prior written consent of the publisher or a license from
The Canadian Copyright Licensing Agency (Access Copyright). For an
Access Copyright license, visit www.accesscopyright.ca or call toll free
to 1-800-893-5777.

Groundwood Books / House of Anansi Press
groundwoodbooks.com

We gratefully acknowledge for their financial support of our
publishing program the Canada Council for the Arts, the Ontario Arts
Council and the Government of Canada.

Library and Archives Canada Cataloguing in Publication
Title: The playgrounds of Babel / JonArno Lawson ; [illustrations by]
Piet Grobler.
Names: Lawson, JonArno, author. | Grobler, Piet, illustrator.
Identifiers: Canadiana (print) 20189065540 | Canadiana (ebook)
20189065559 | ISBN 9781773060361 (hardcover) | ISBN
9781773060378 (EPUB) | ISBN 9781773062778 (Kindle)
Classification: LCC PS8573.A93 P53 2019 | DDC jC813/.54—dc23

The art was created with gouache, collage, ink and color pencils.
Design by Michael Solomon
Printed and bound in China

Canada Council   Conseil des Arts
for the Arts   du Canada

ONTARIO ARTS COUNCIL
CONSEIL DES ARTS DE L'ONTARIO
an Ontario government agency
un organisme du gouvernement de l'Ontario

With the participation of the Government of Canada | Canada
Avec la participation du gouvernement du Canada

FSC
www.fsc.org
MIX
Paper from
responsible sources
FSC® C144853

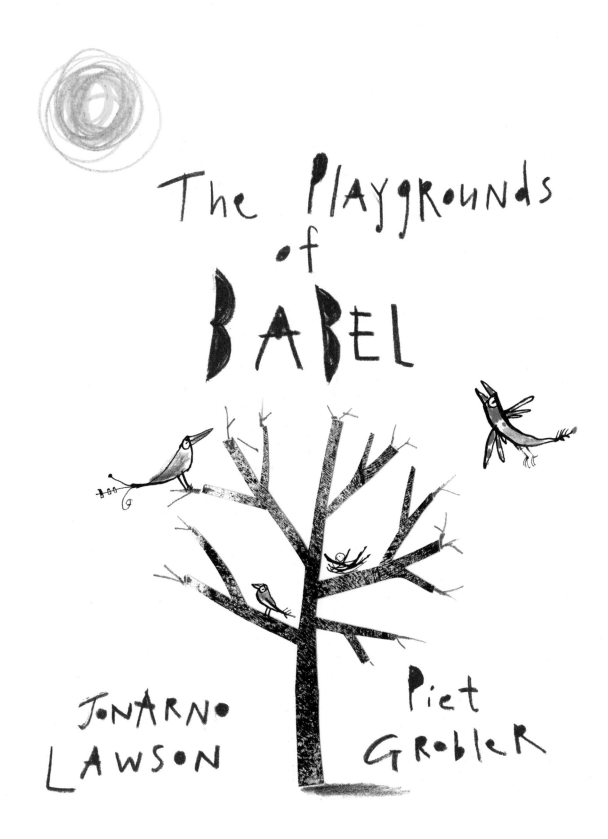

The Playgrounds of BABEL

JonArno Lawson

Piet Grobler

 Groundwood Books
House of Anansi Press
Toronto Berkeley

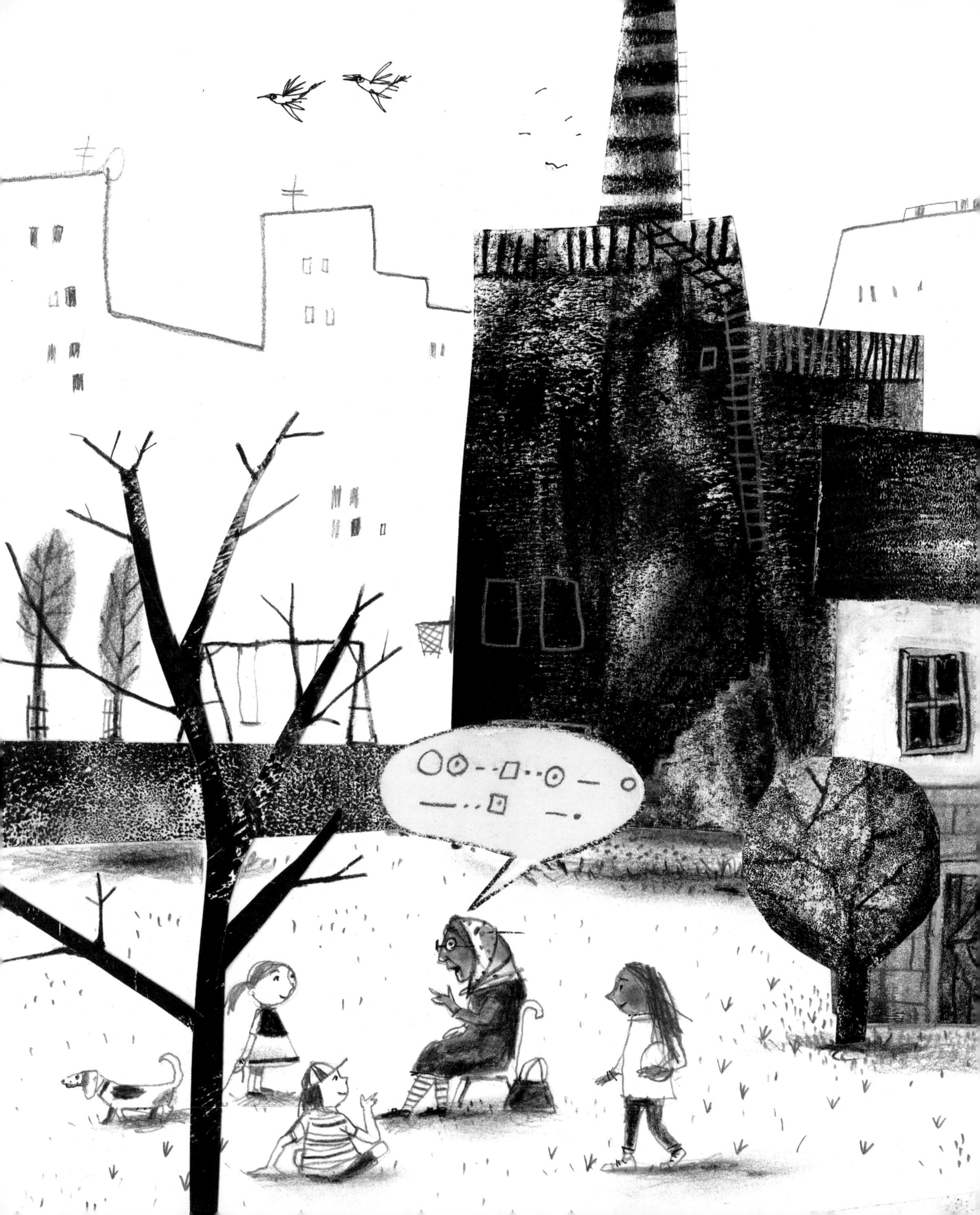

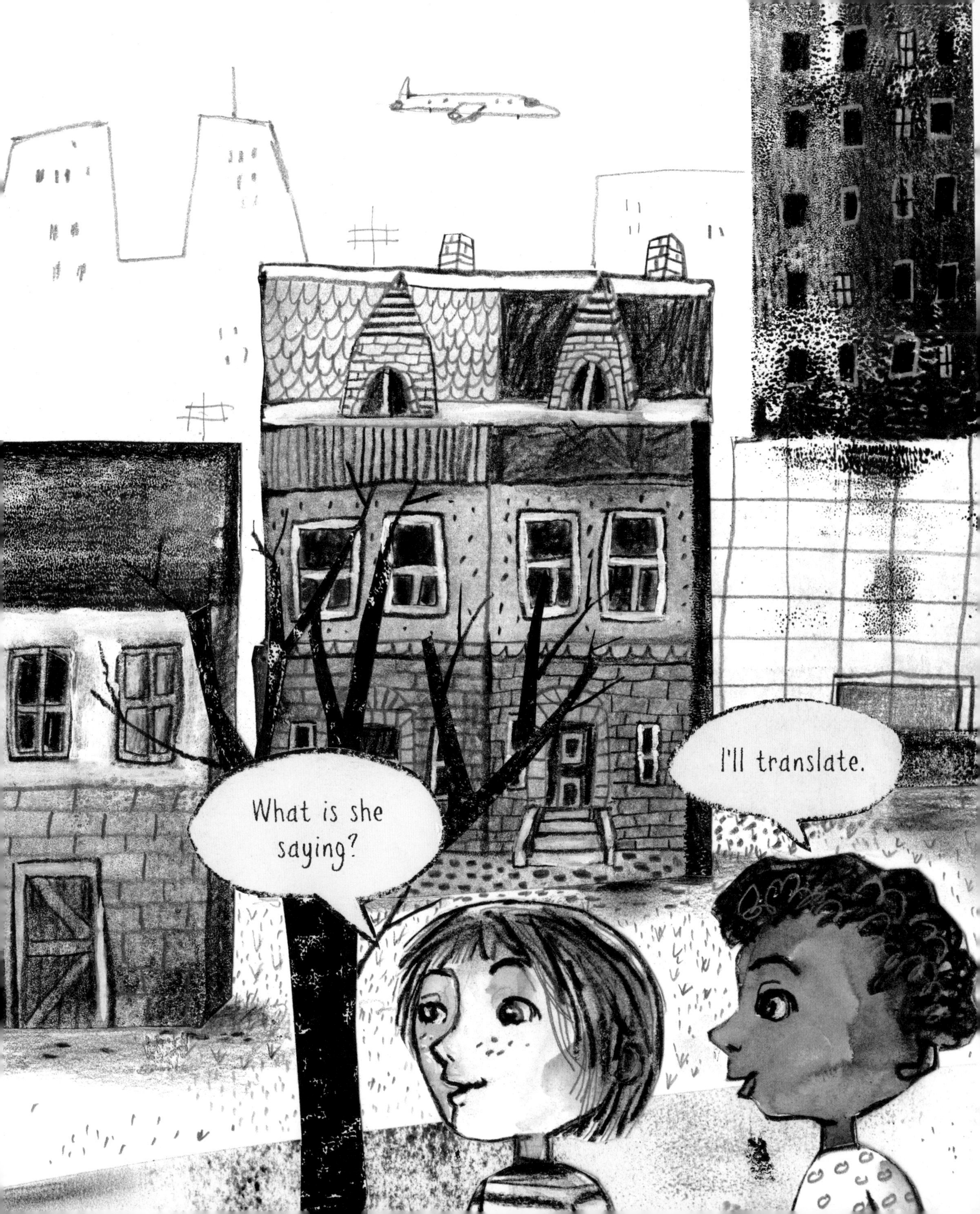
What is she saying?
I'll translate.

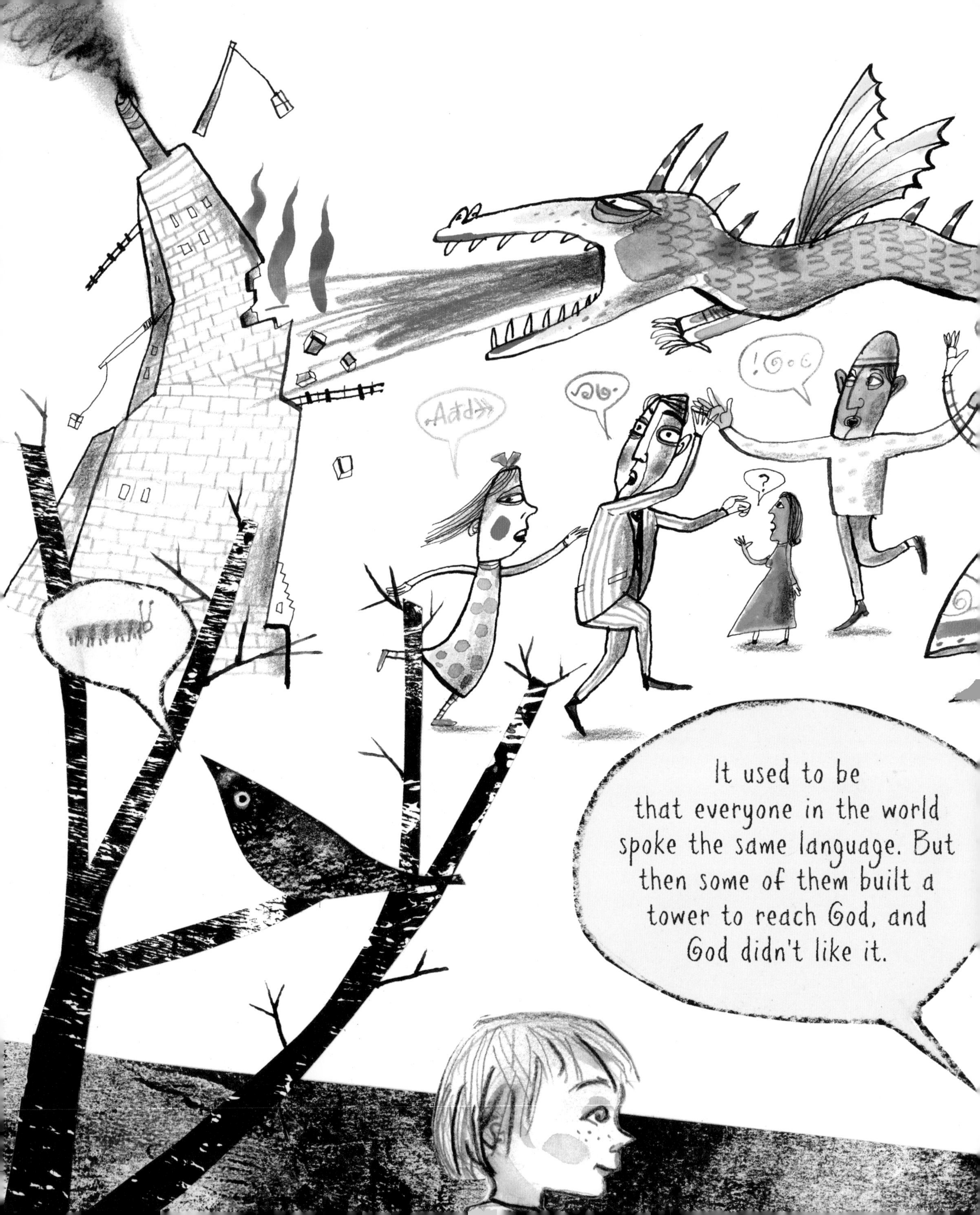
?
It used to be that everyone in the world spoke the same language. But then some of them built a tower to reach God, and God didn't like it.

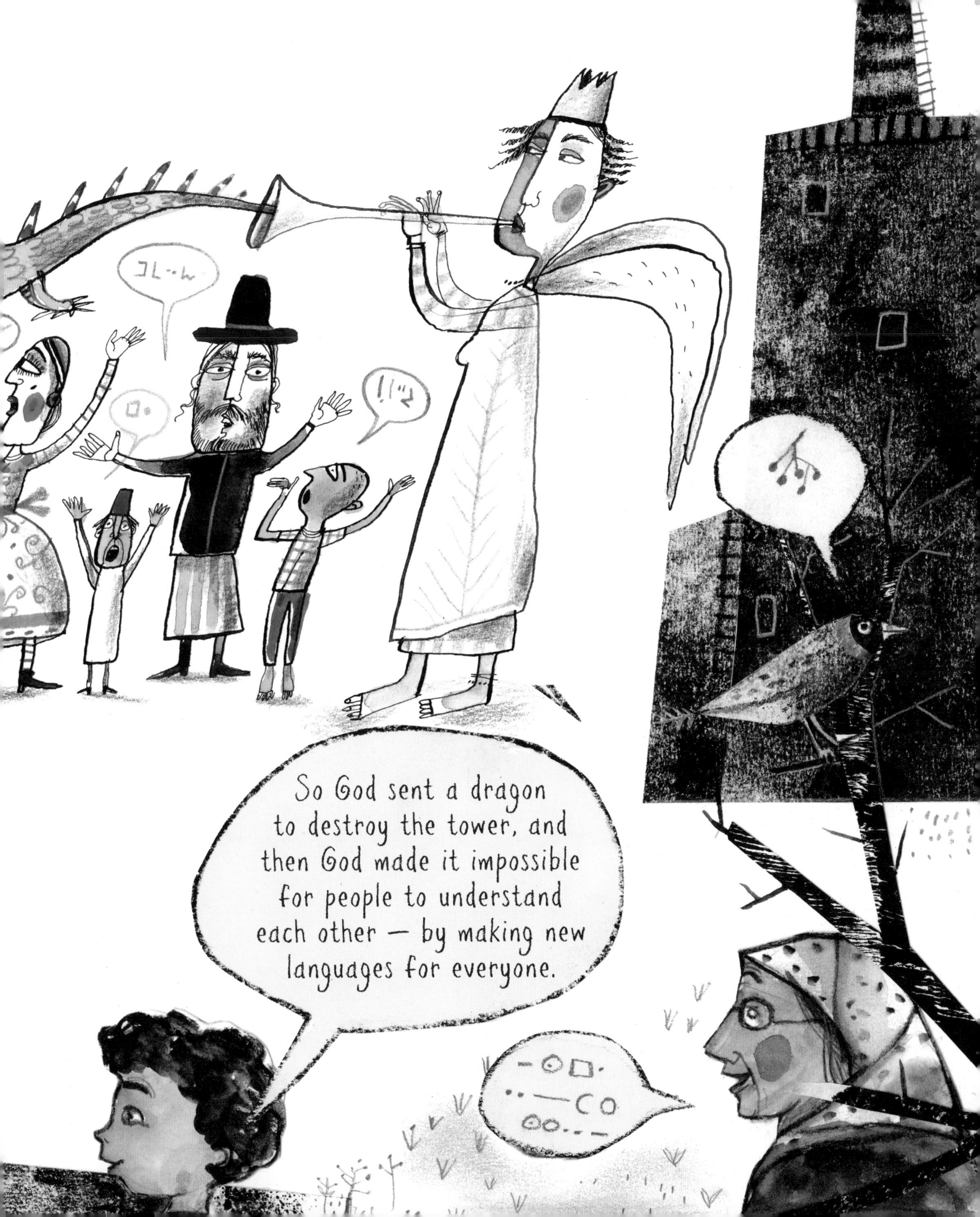
So God sent a dragon to destroy the tower, and then God made it impossible for people to understand each other — by making new languages for everyone.

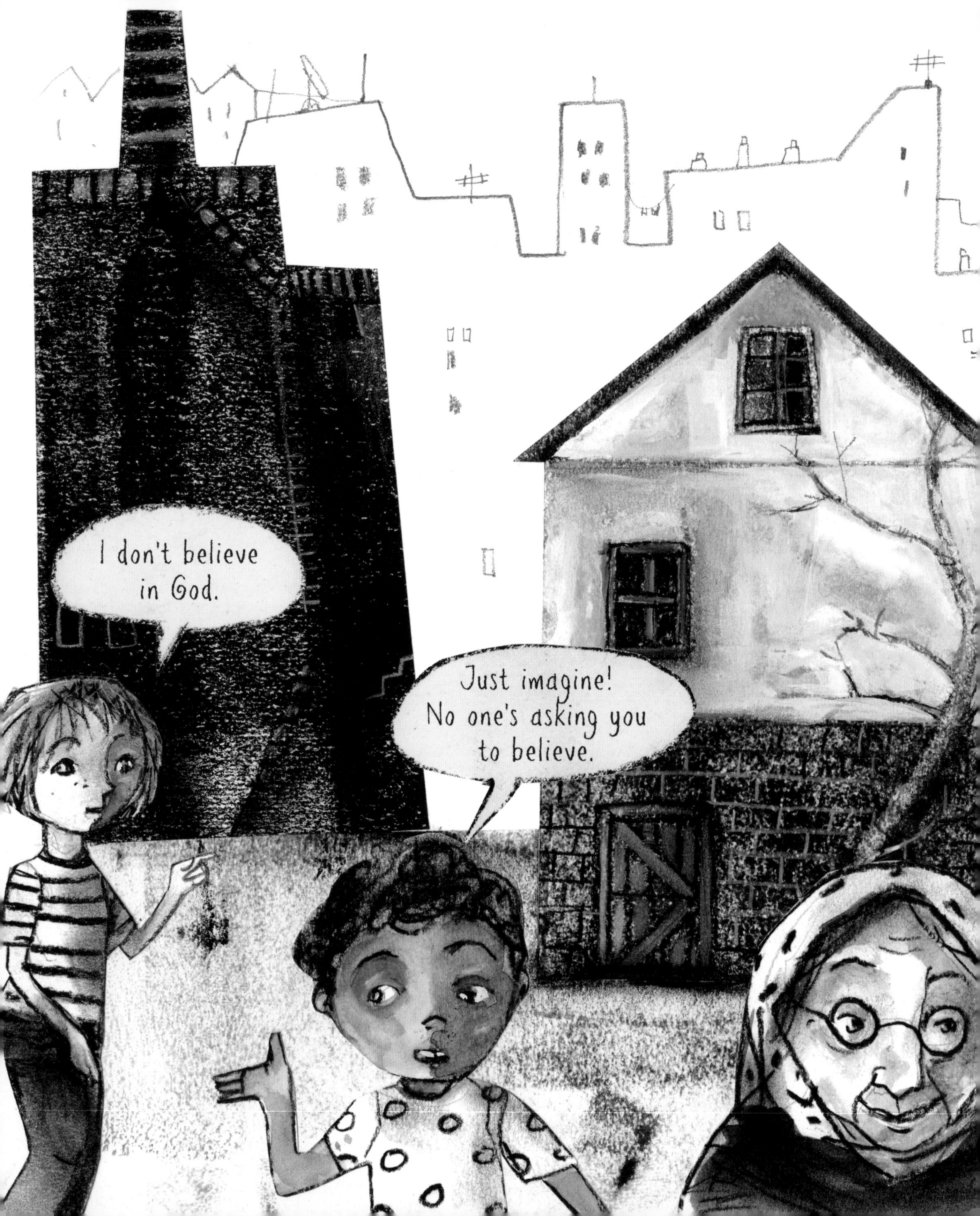
I don't believe in God.
Just imagine! No one's asking you to believe.

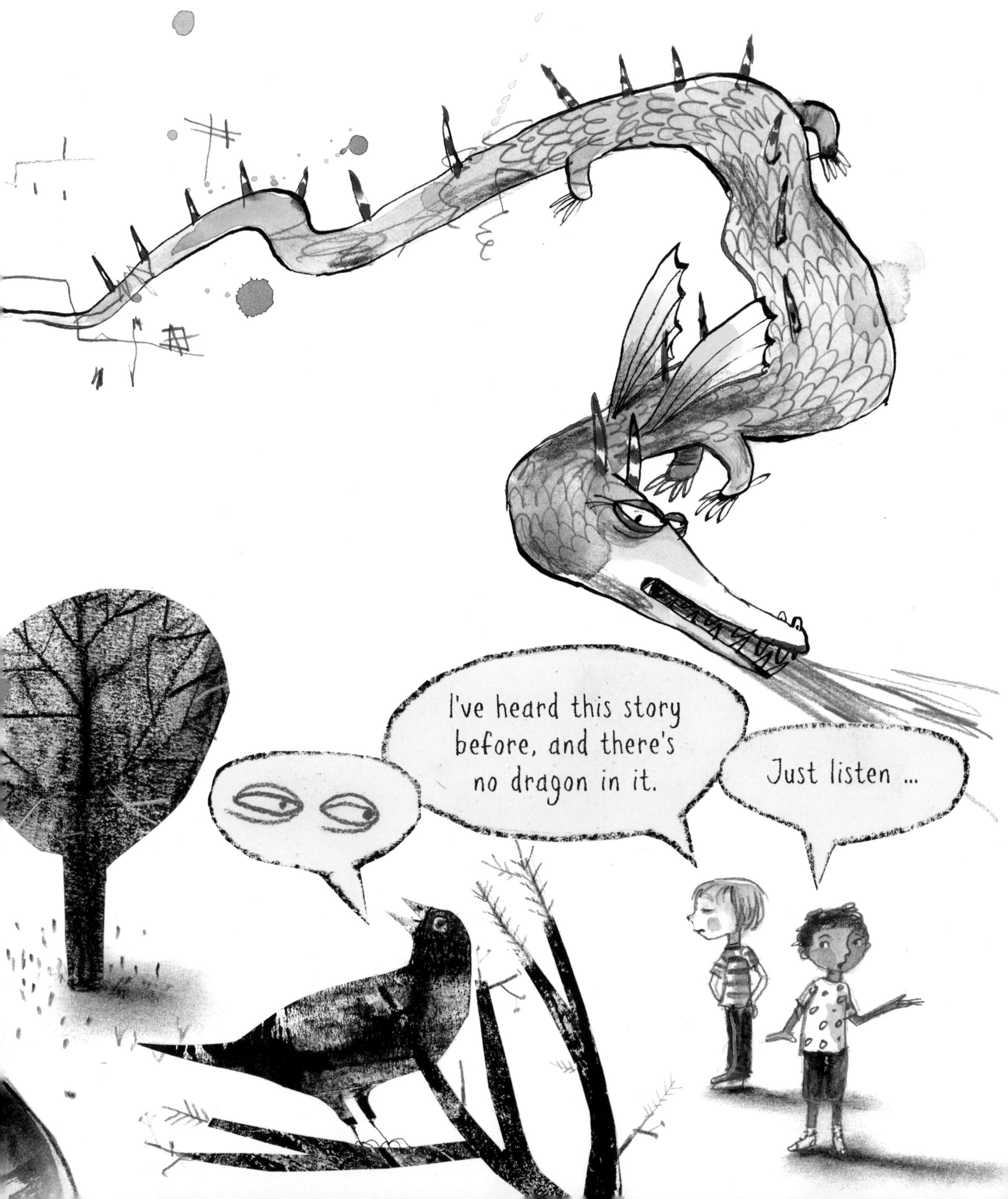
I've heard this story before, and there's no dragon in it.
Just listen ...

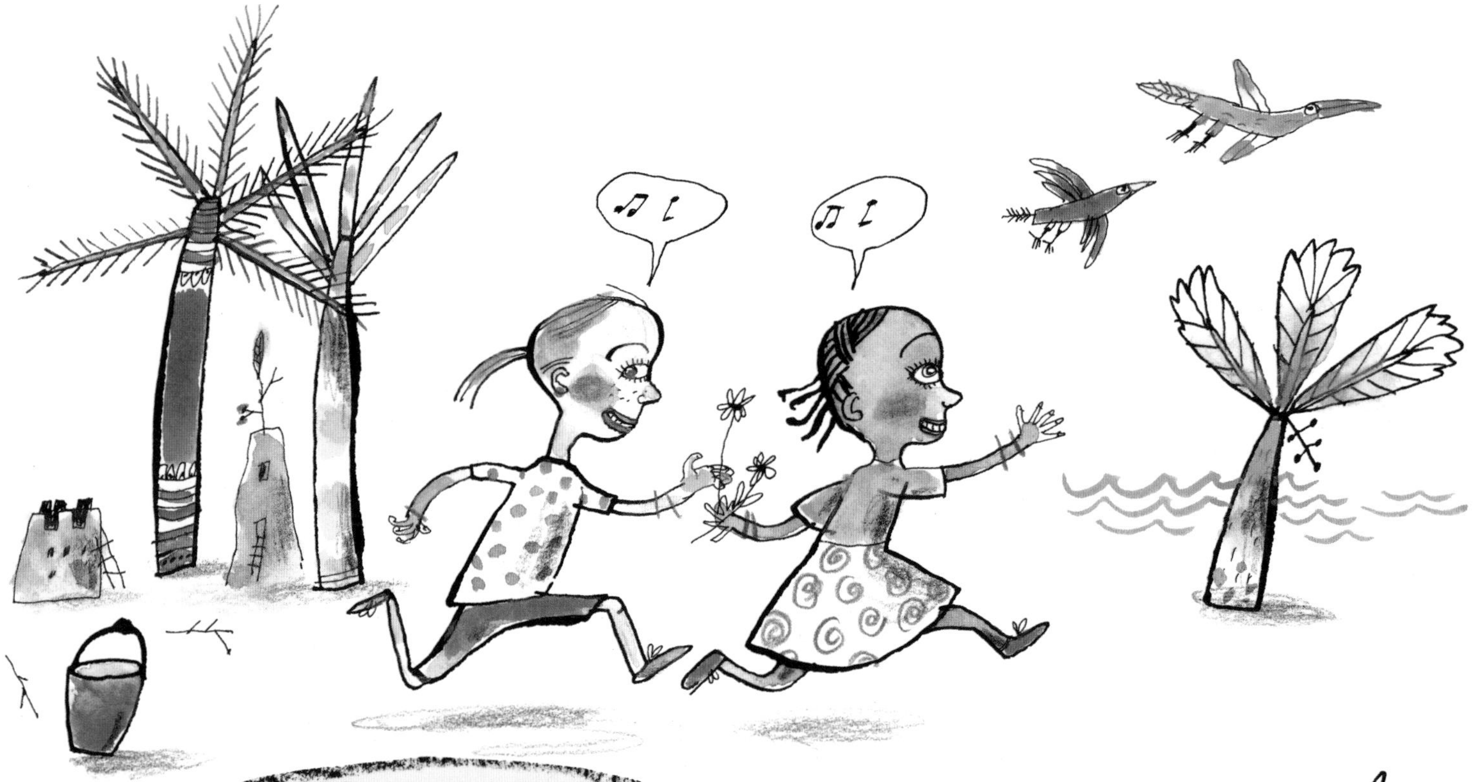

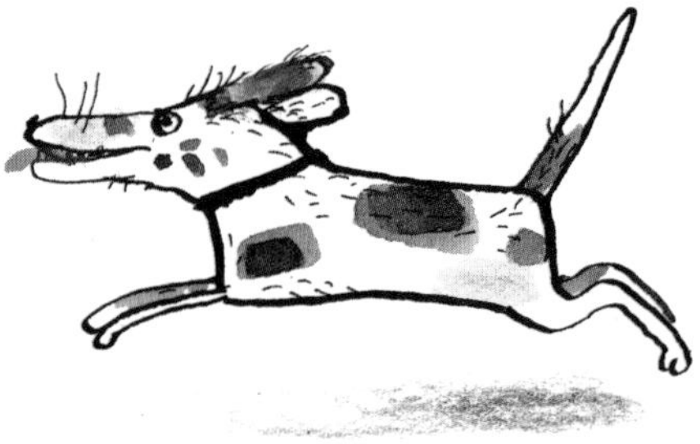

There were two girls who were good friends. They played together and sang together — they did everything together.

What a catastrophe when suddenly — out of the blue — they couldn't speak to each other! Between one handclap and the next, they were speaking different languages.

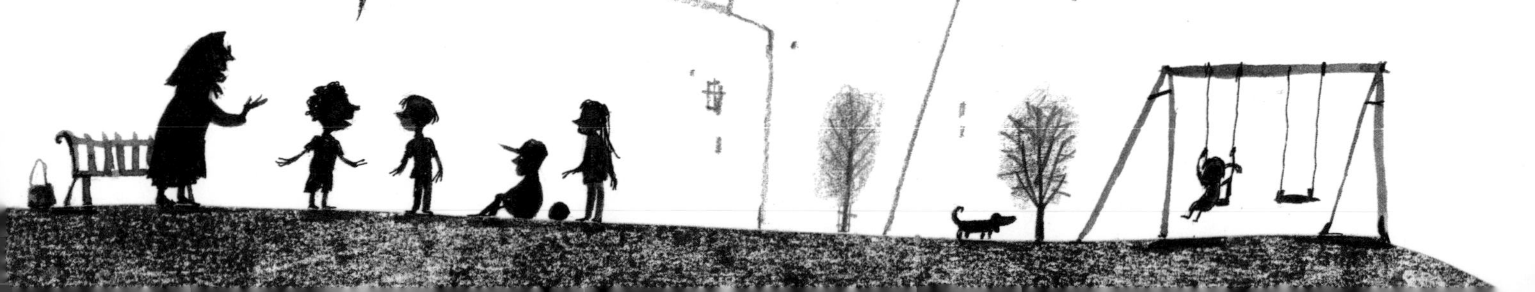

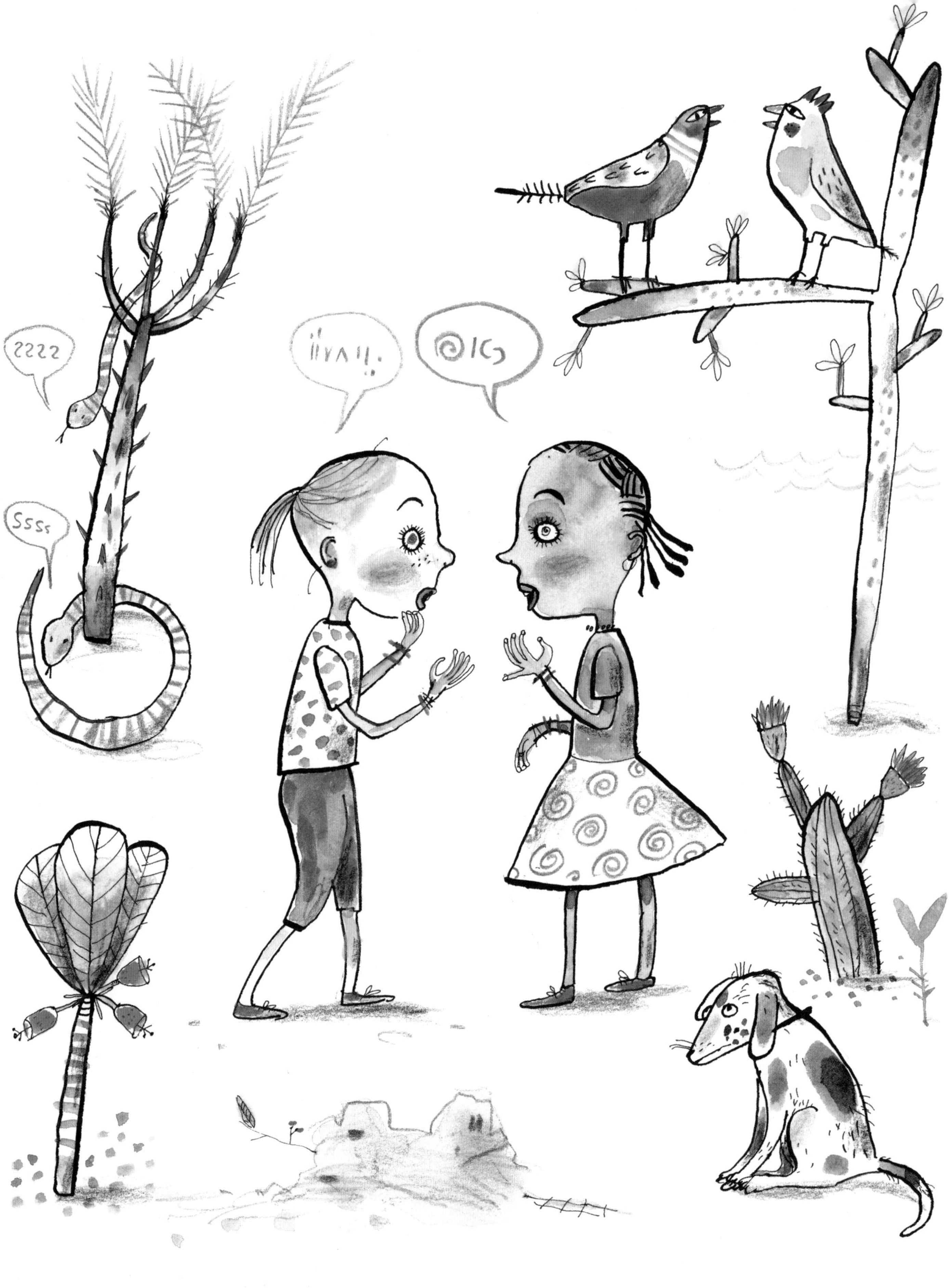
zzzz
Ssss

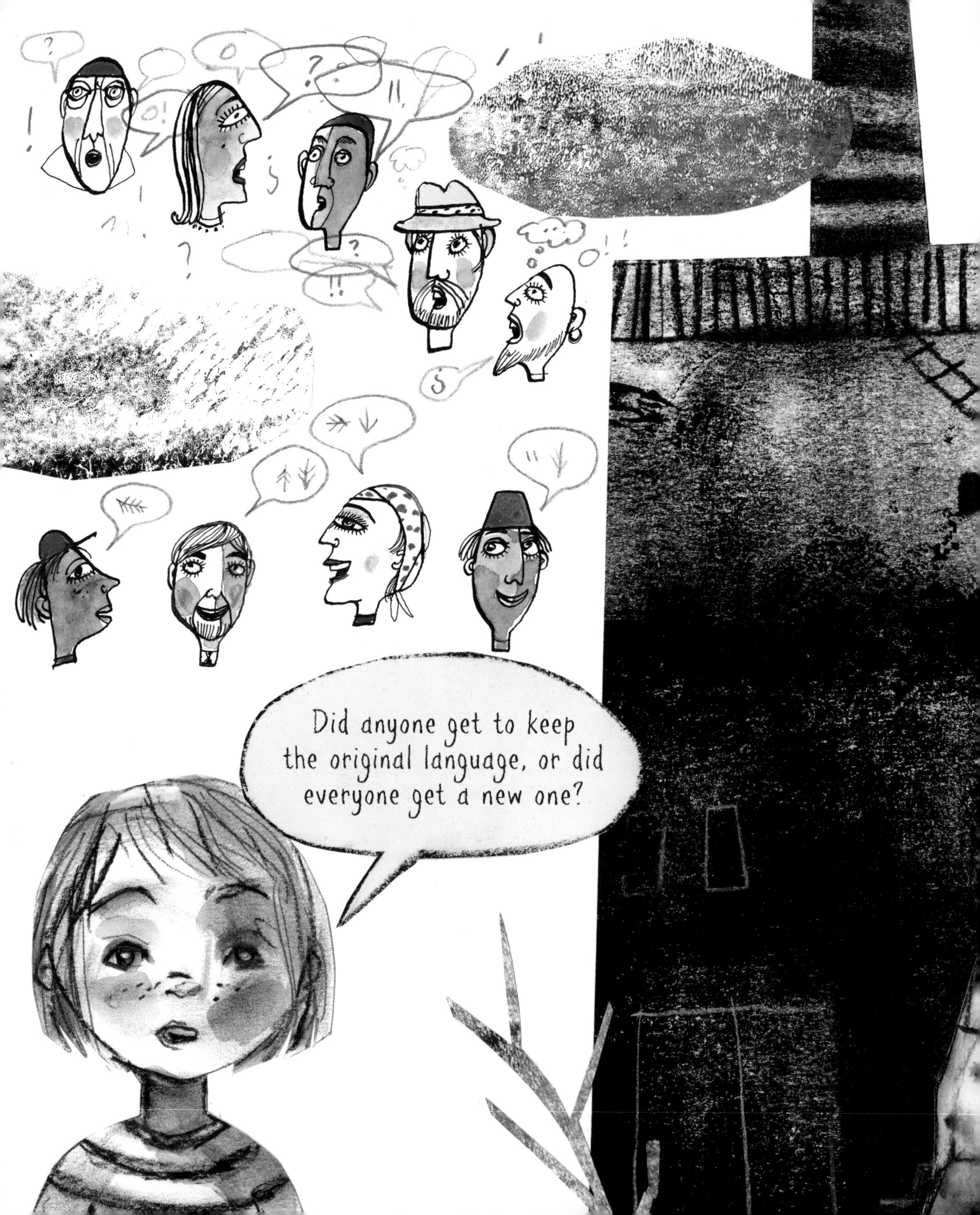
Did anyone get to keep the original language, or did everyone get a new one?

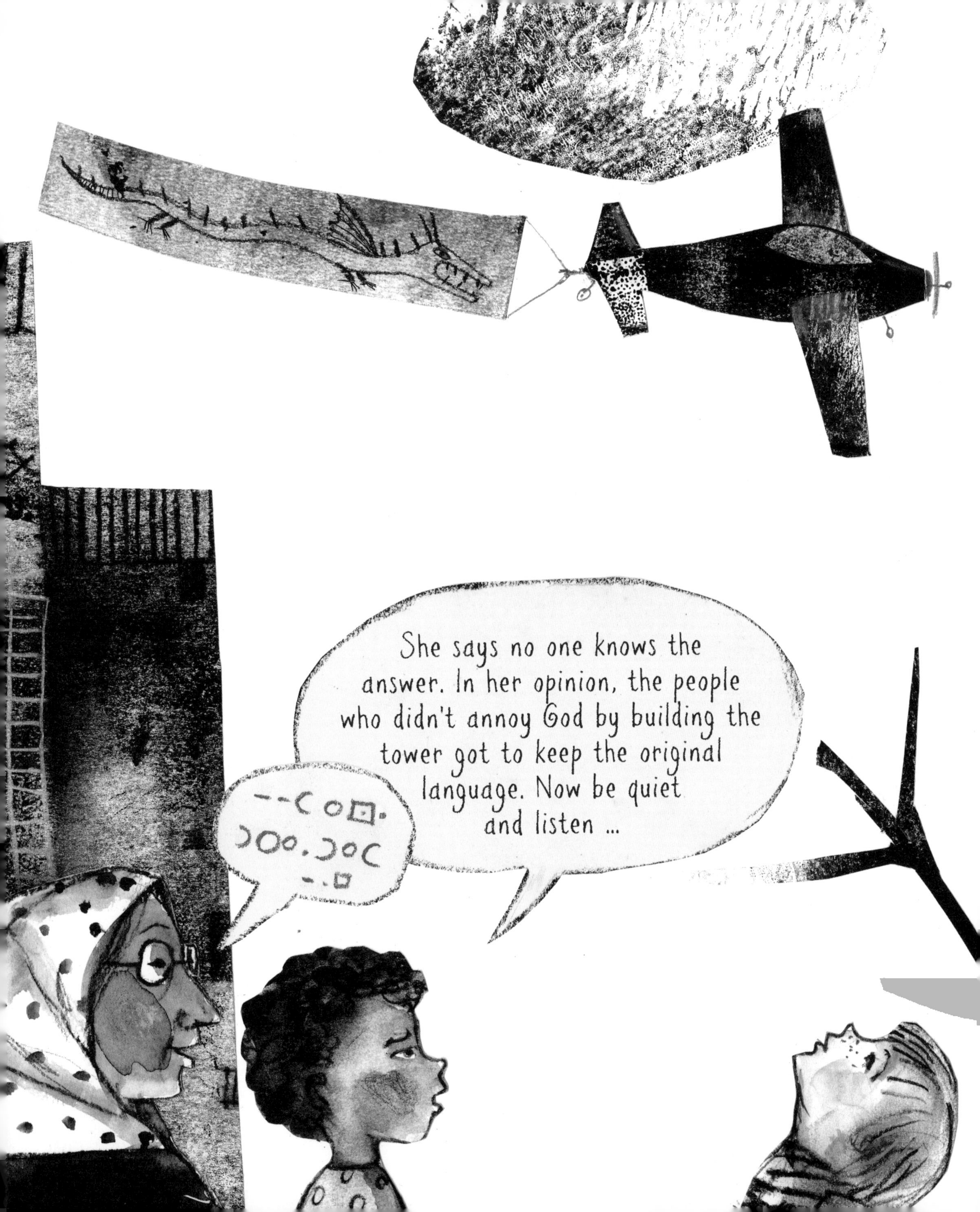
She says no one knows the answer. In her opinion, the people who didn't annoy God by building the tower got to keep the original language. Now be quiet and listen ...

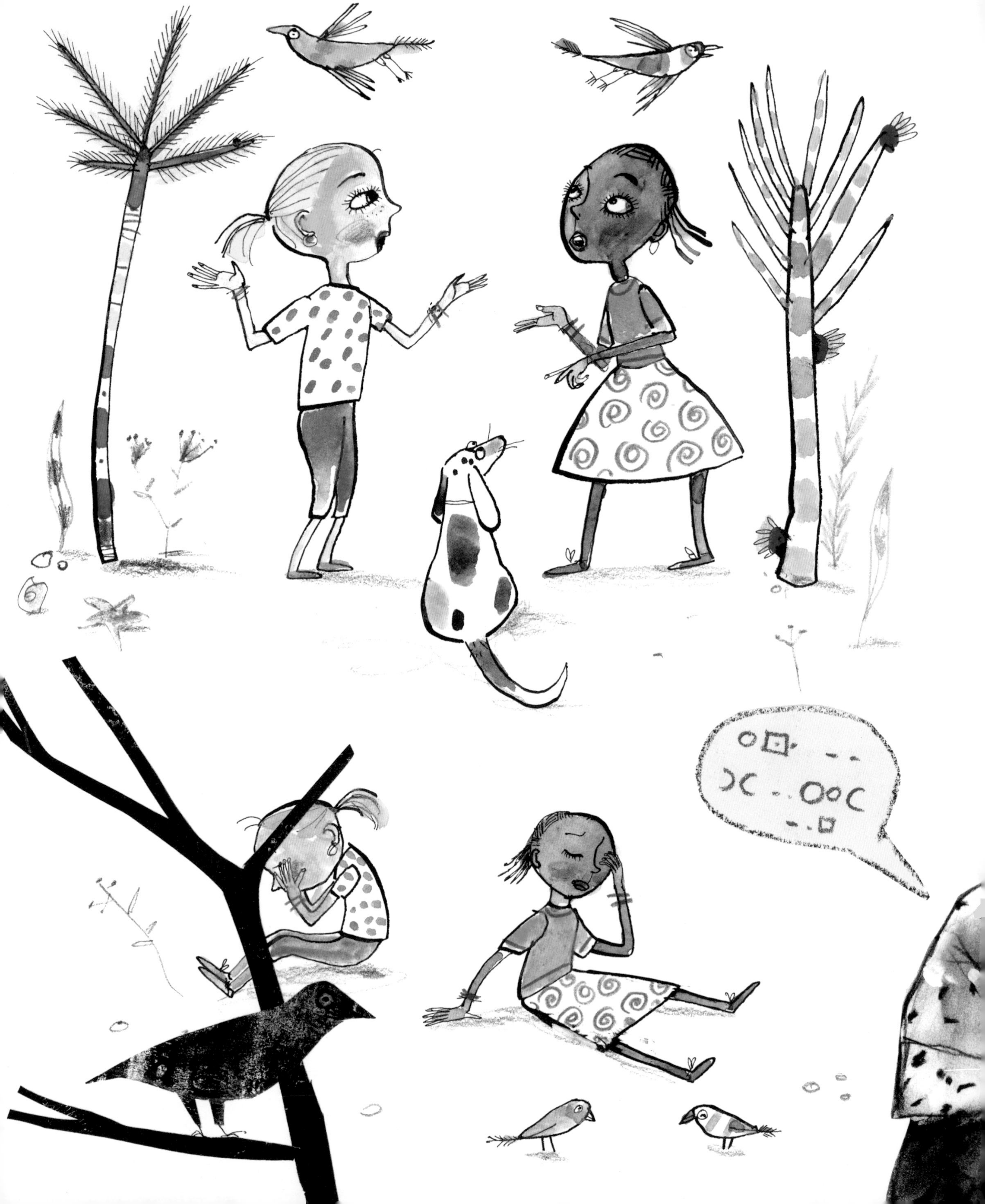

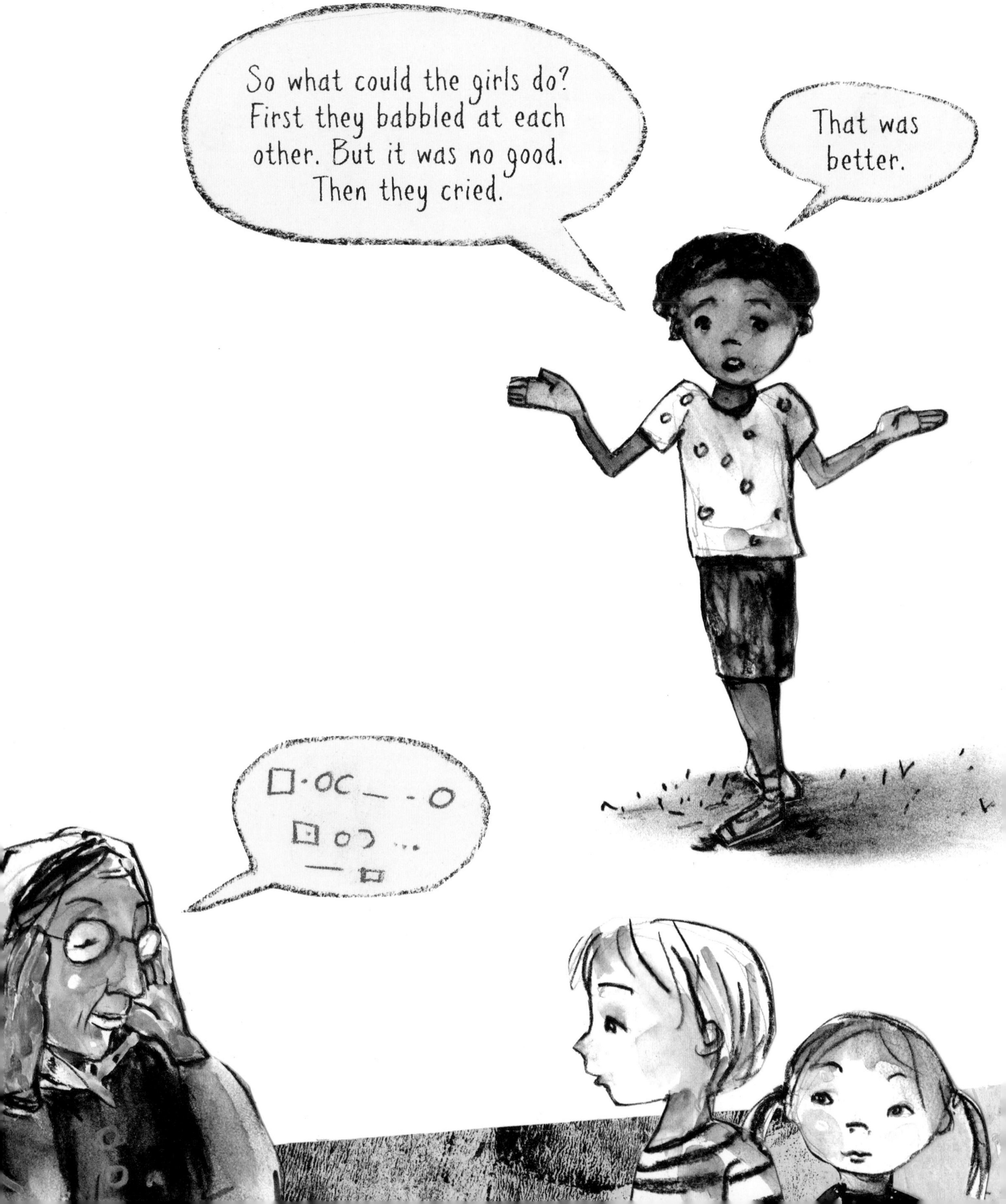
So what could the girls do? First they babbled at each other. But it was no good. Then they cried.
That was better.

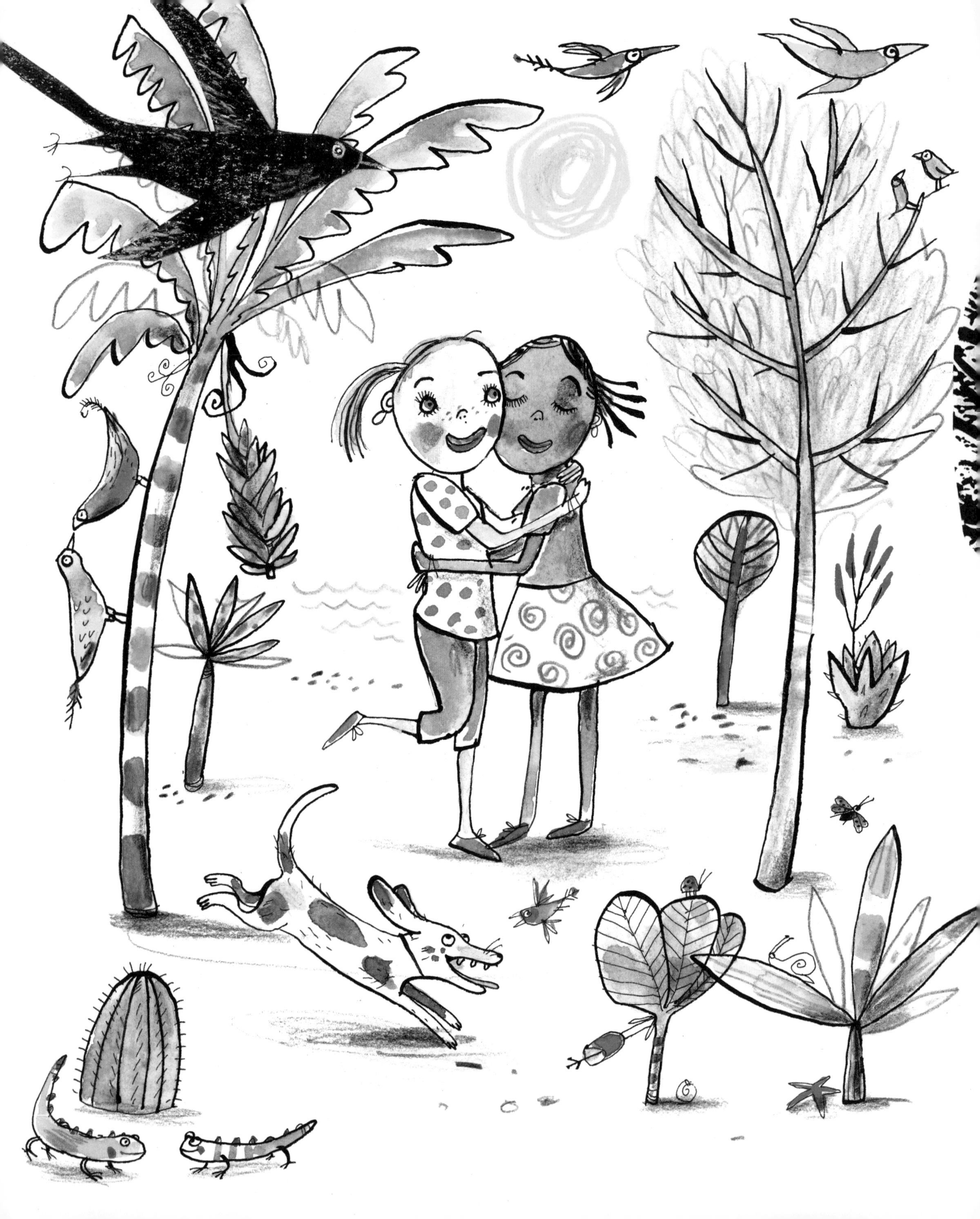

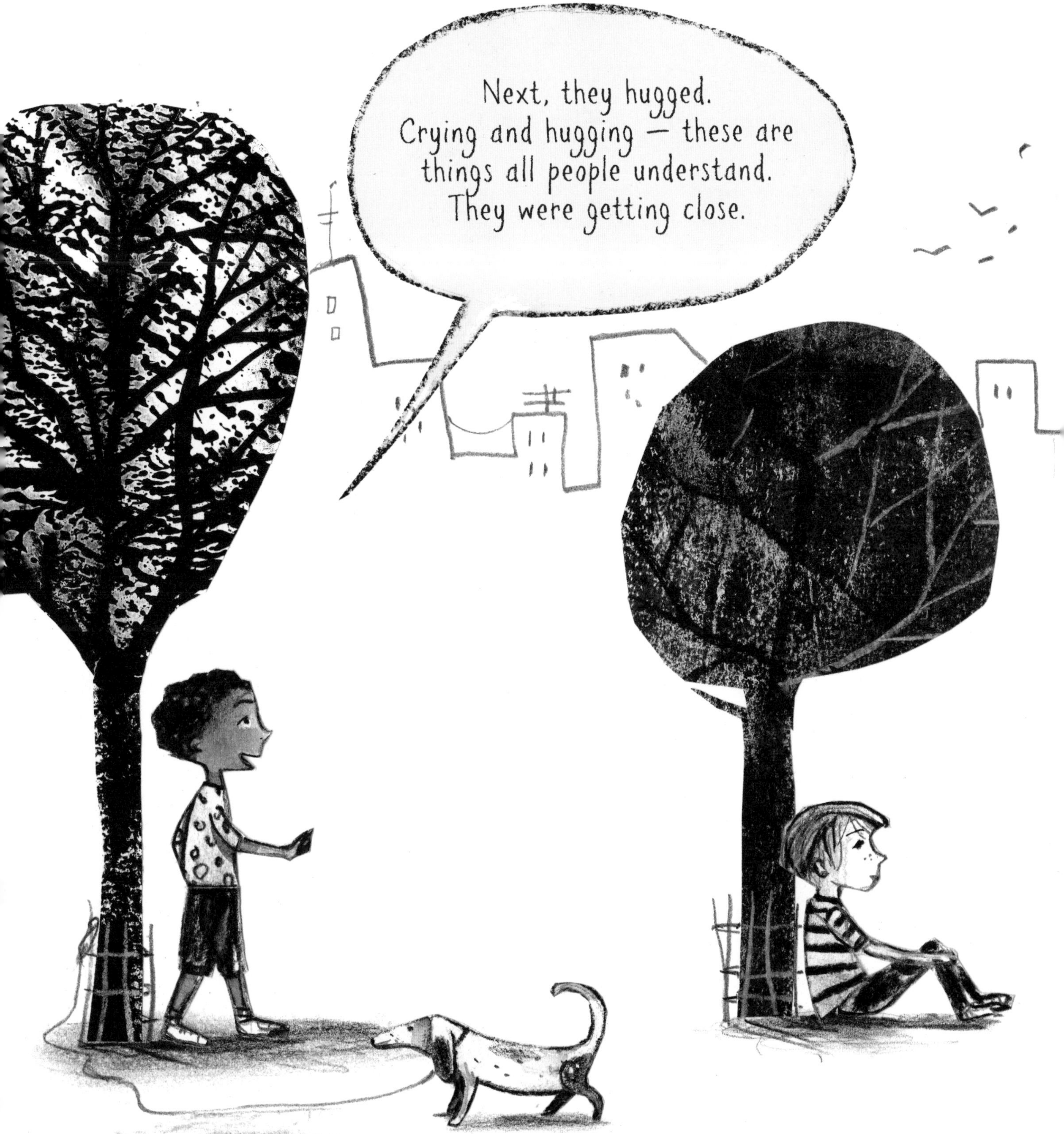
Next, they hugged. Crying and hugging — these are things all people understand. They were getting close.

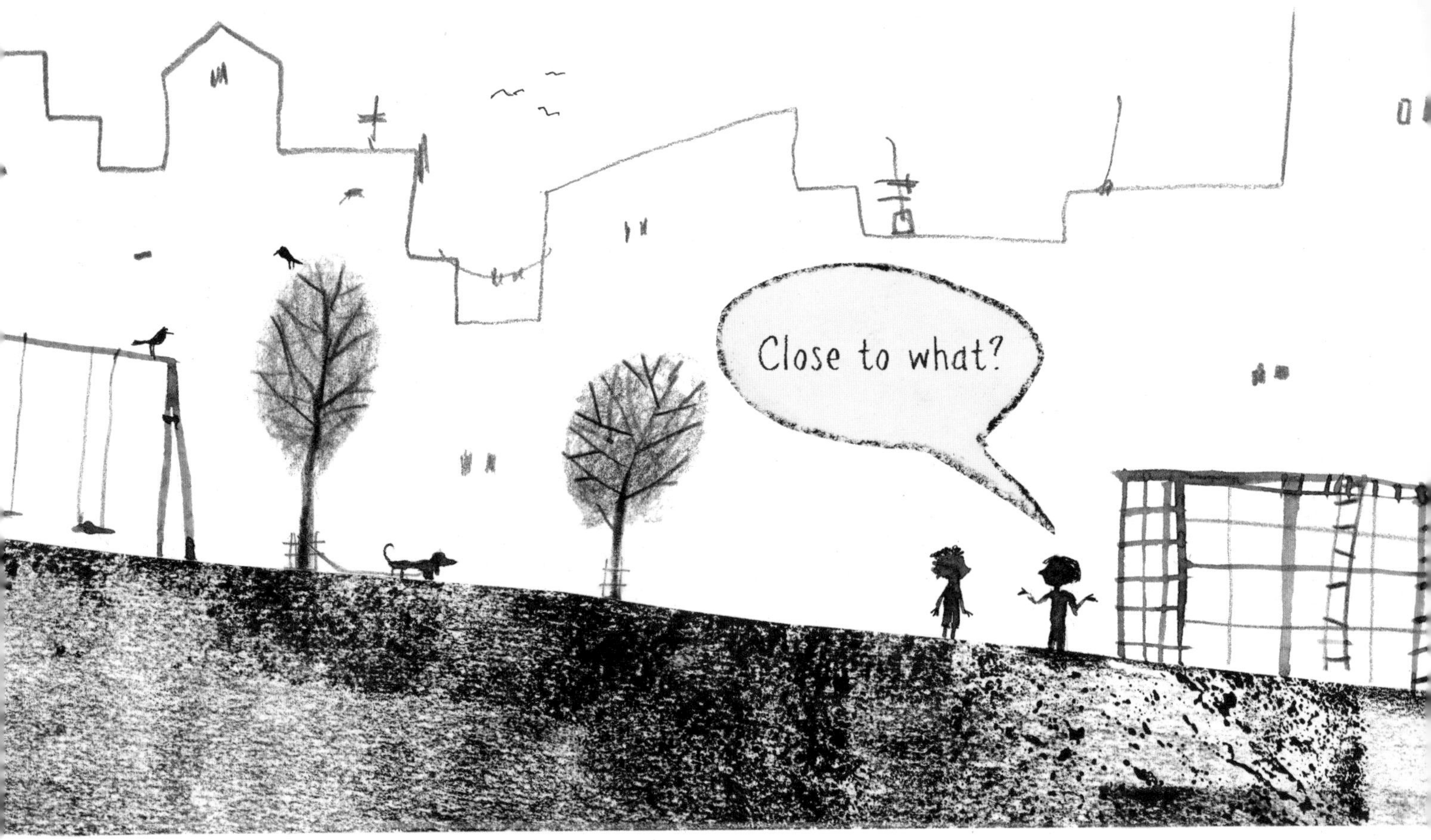
Close to what?

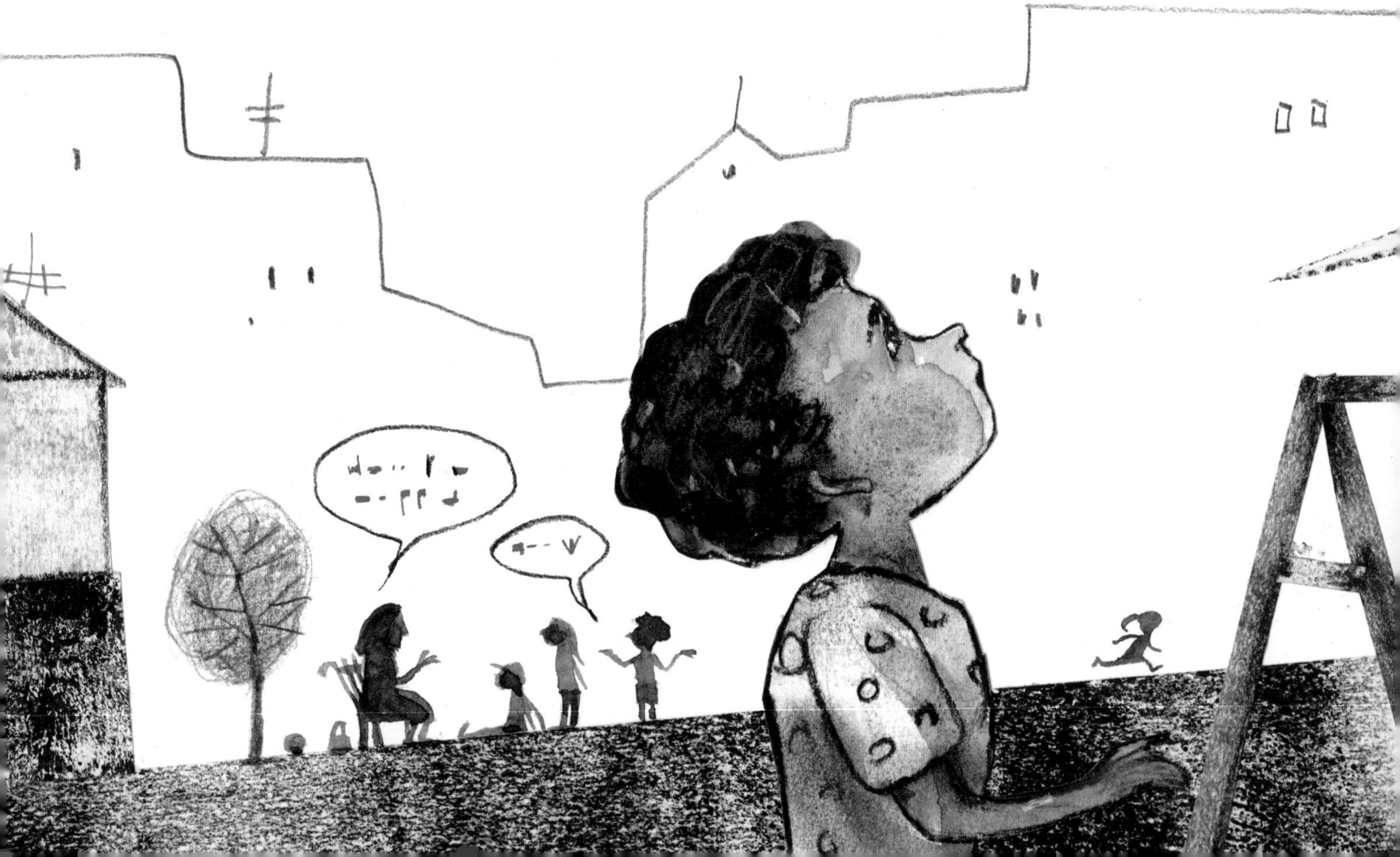

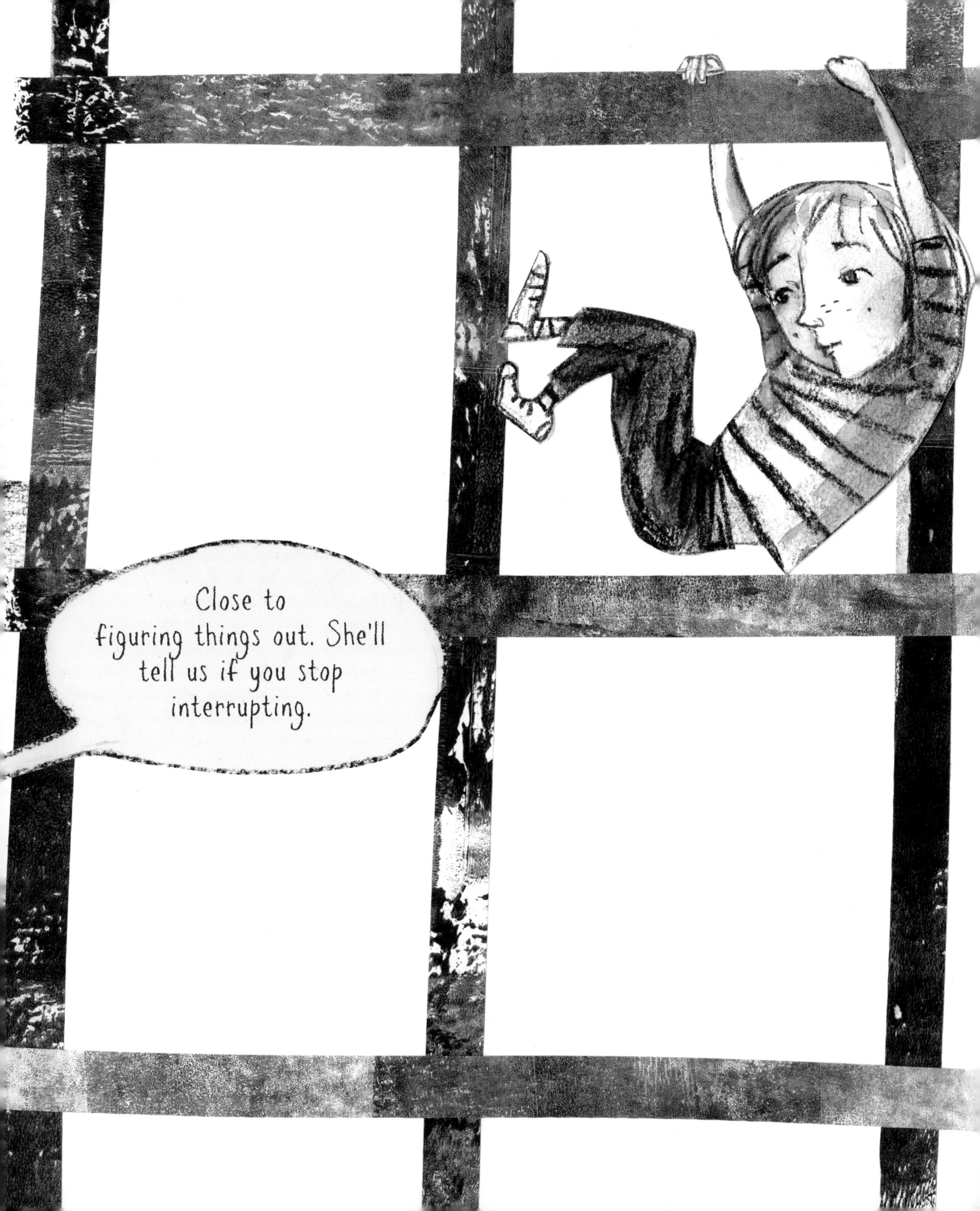
Close to figuring things out. She'll tell us if you stop interrupting.

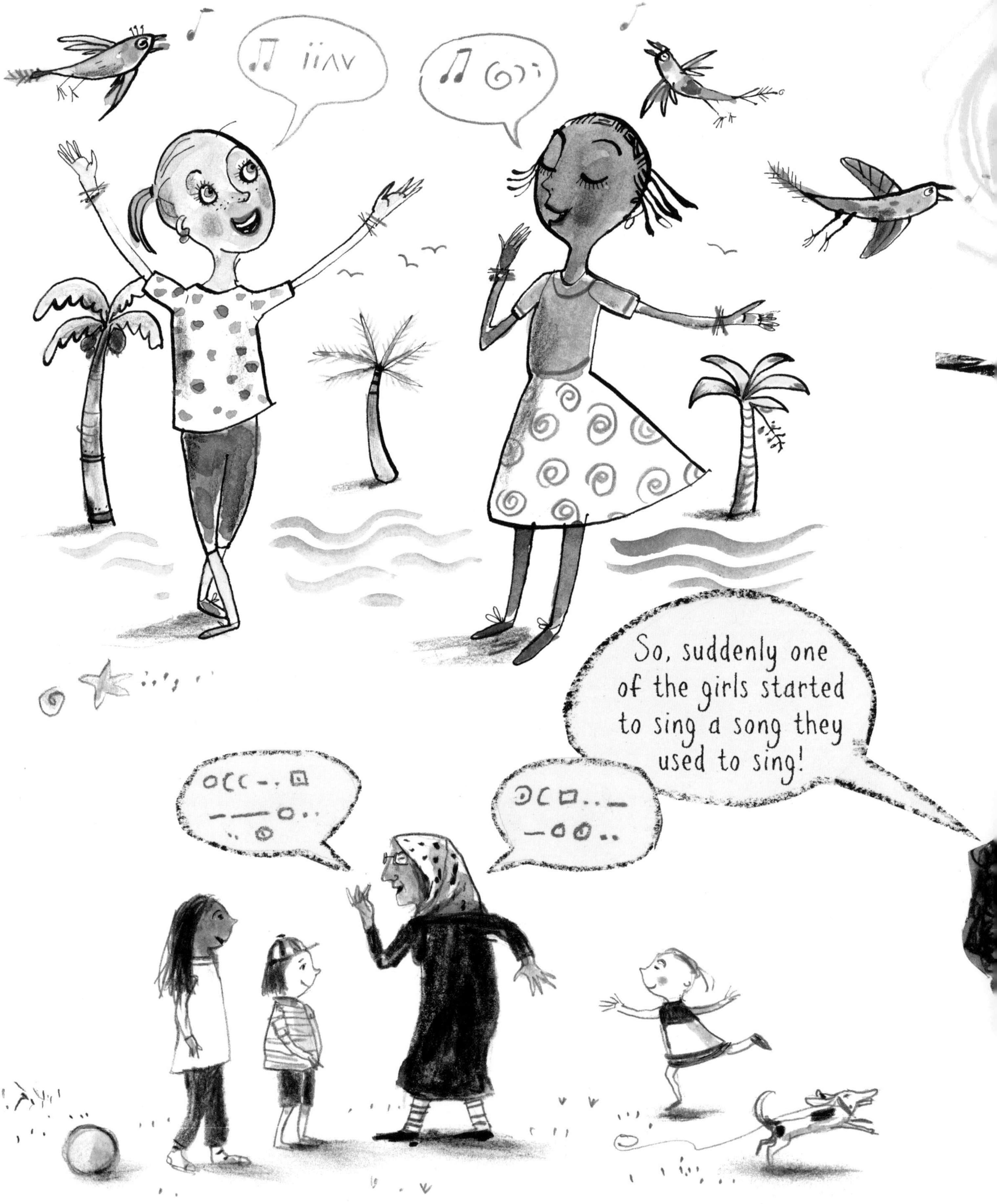
So, suddenly one of the girls started to sing a song they used to sing!

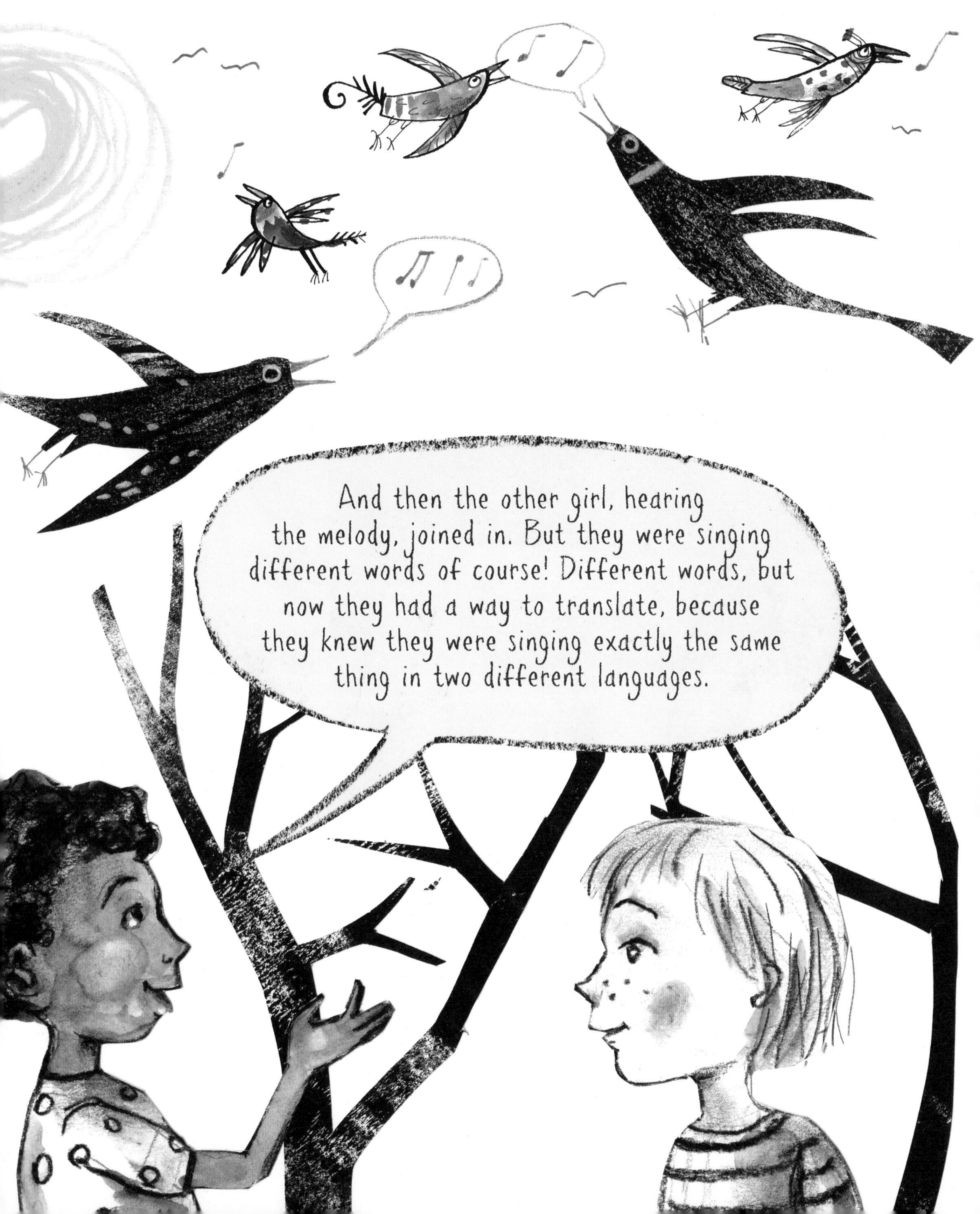
And then the other girl, hearing the melody, joined in. But they were singing different words of course! Different words, but now they had a way to translate, because they knew they were singing exactly the same thing in two different languages.

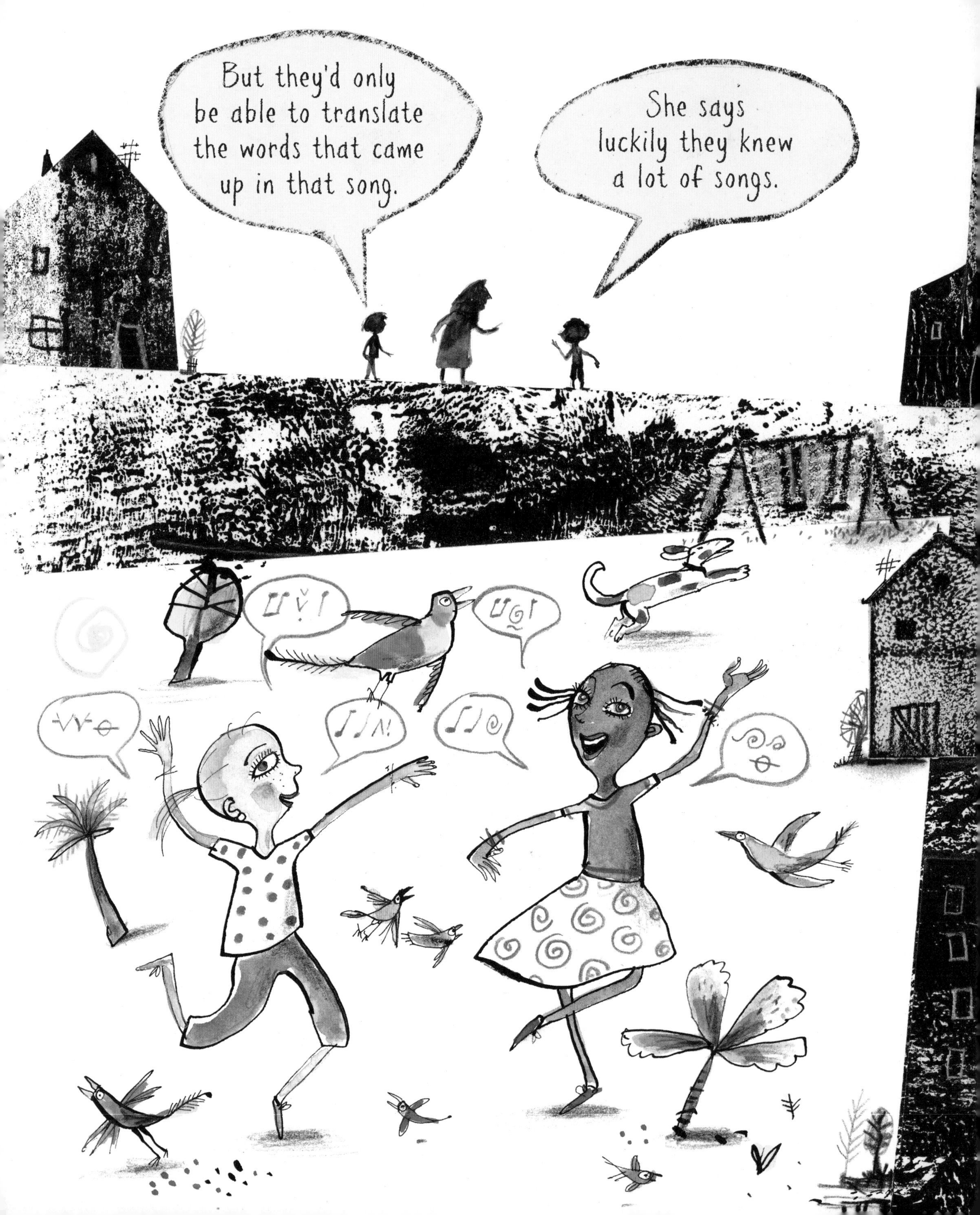
But they'd only be able to translate the words that came up in that song.
She says luckily they knew a lot of songs.

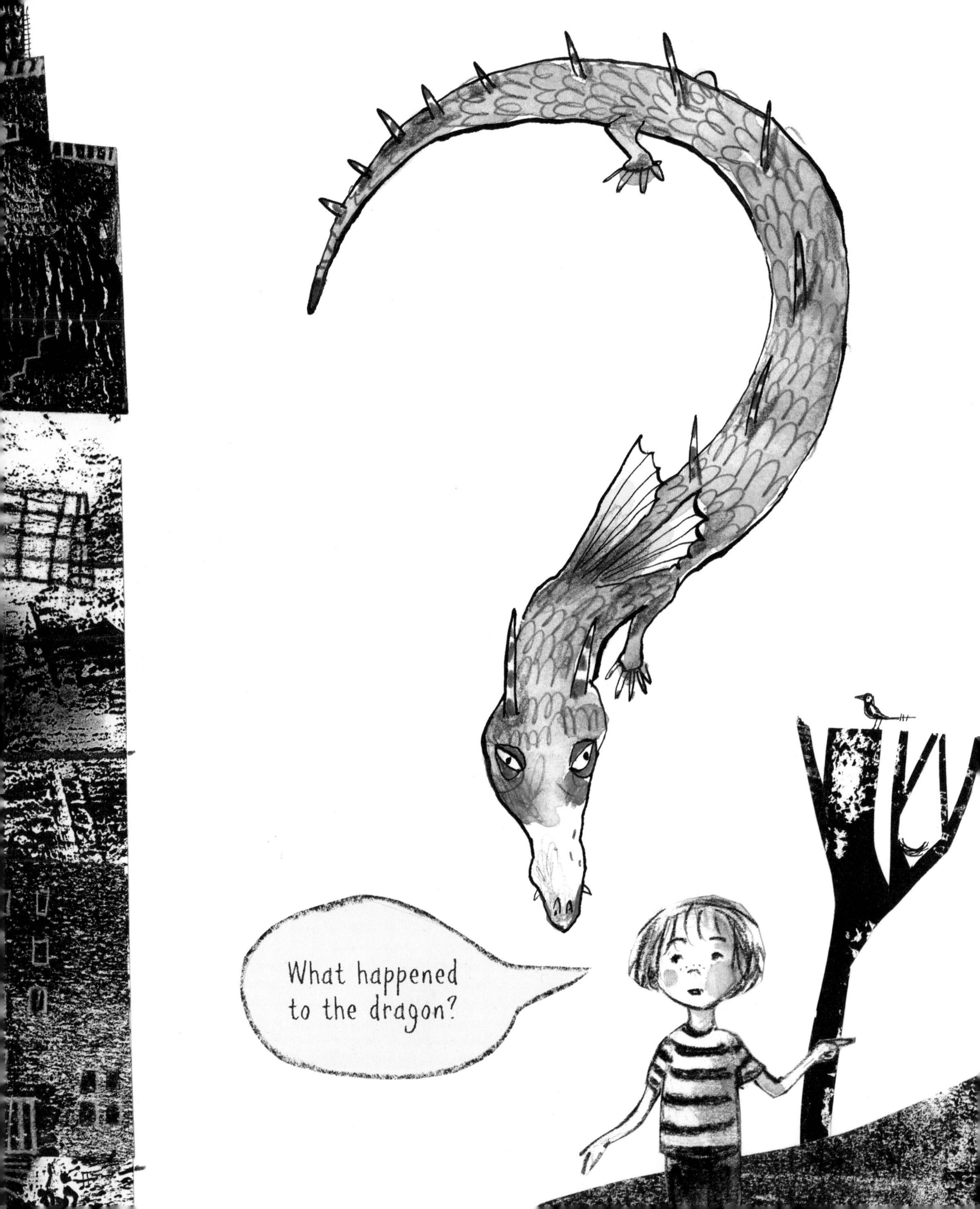
What happened to the dragon?

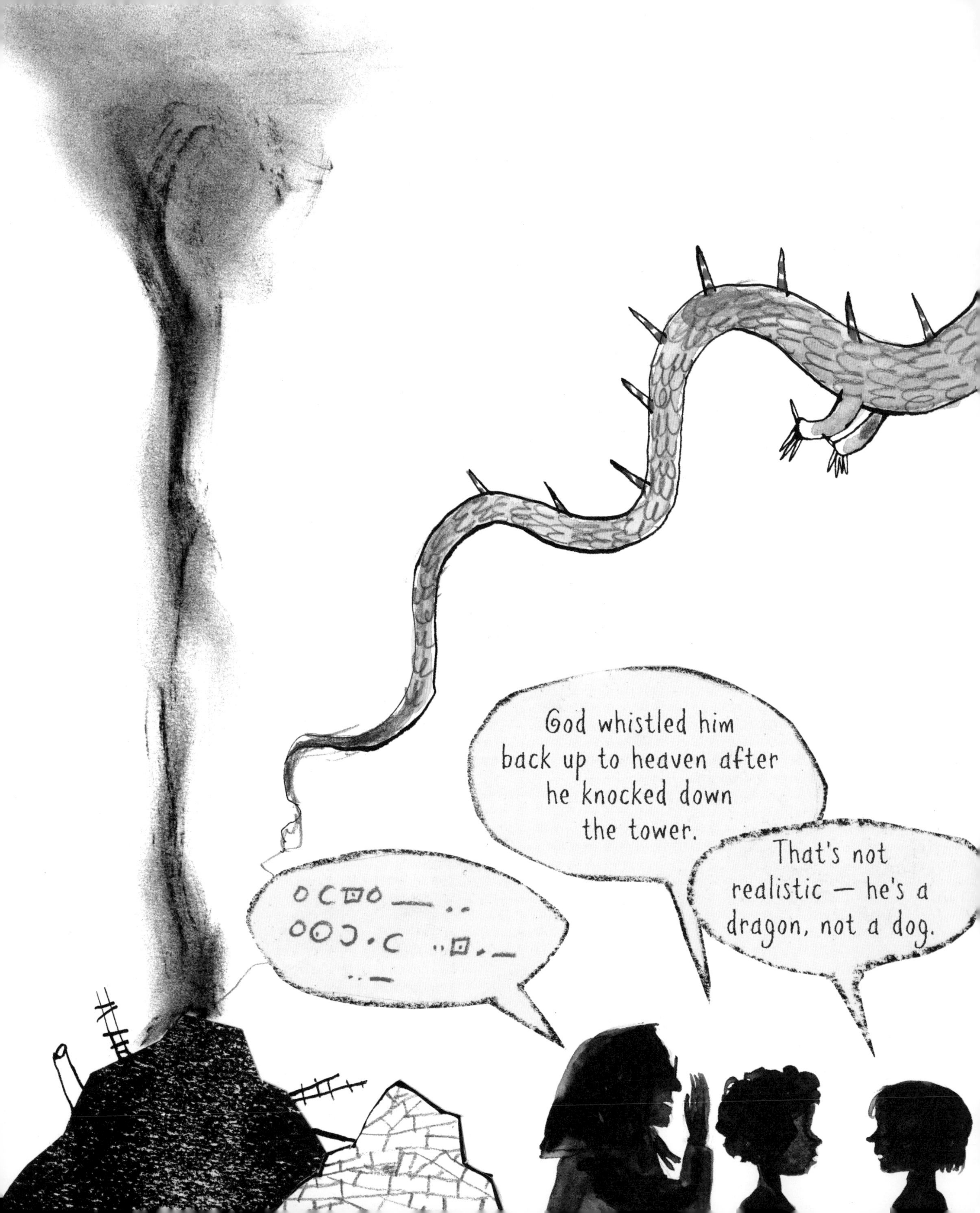
God whistled him back up to heaven after he knocked down the tower.
That's not realistic — he's a dragon, not a dog.

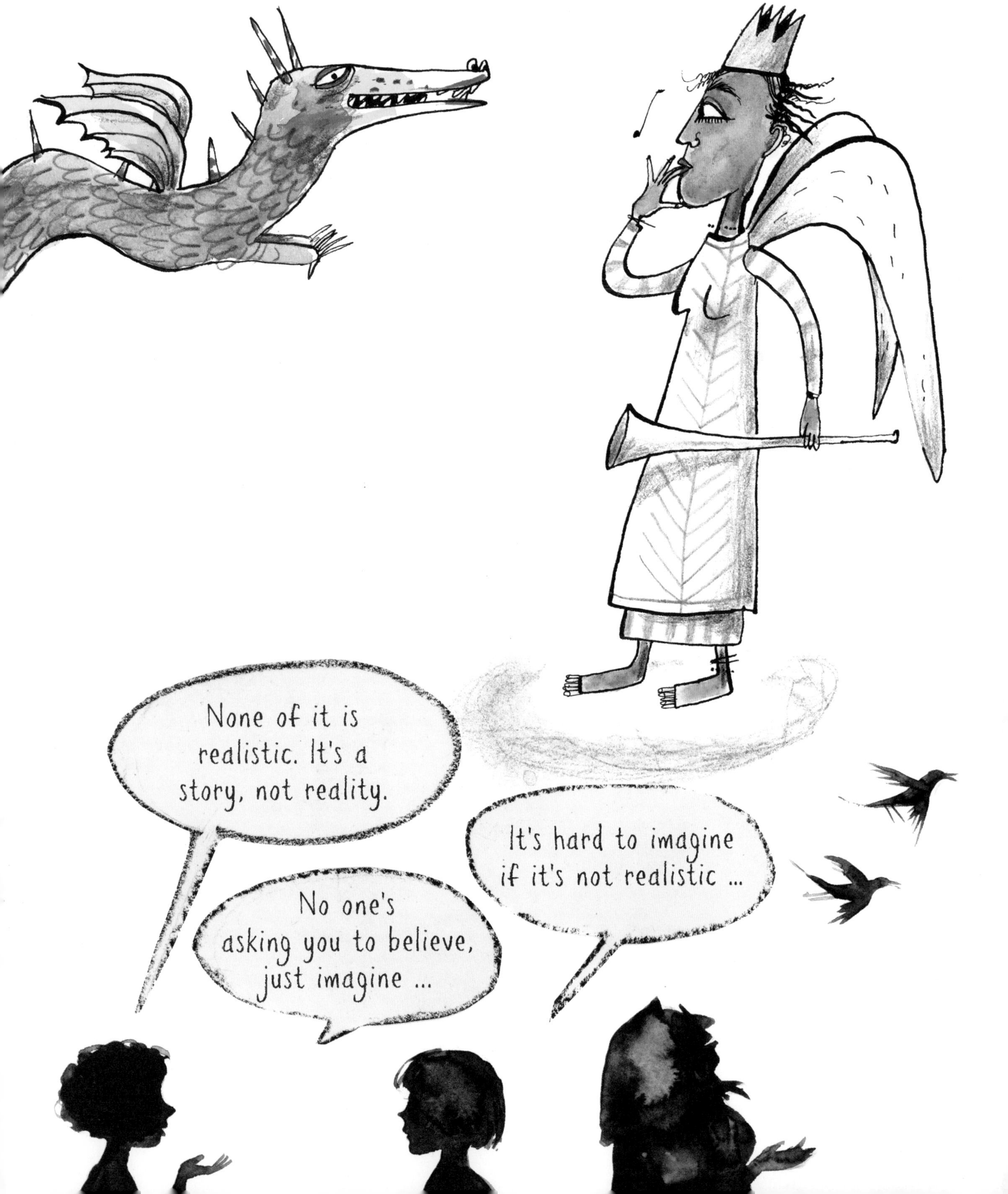
None of it is realistic. It's a story, not reality.
No one's asking you to believe, just imagine ...
It's hard to imagine if it's not realistic ...

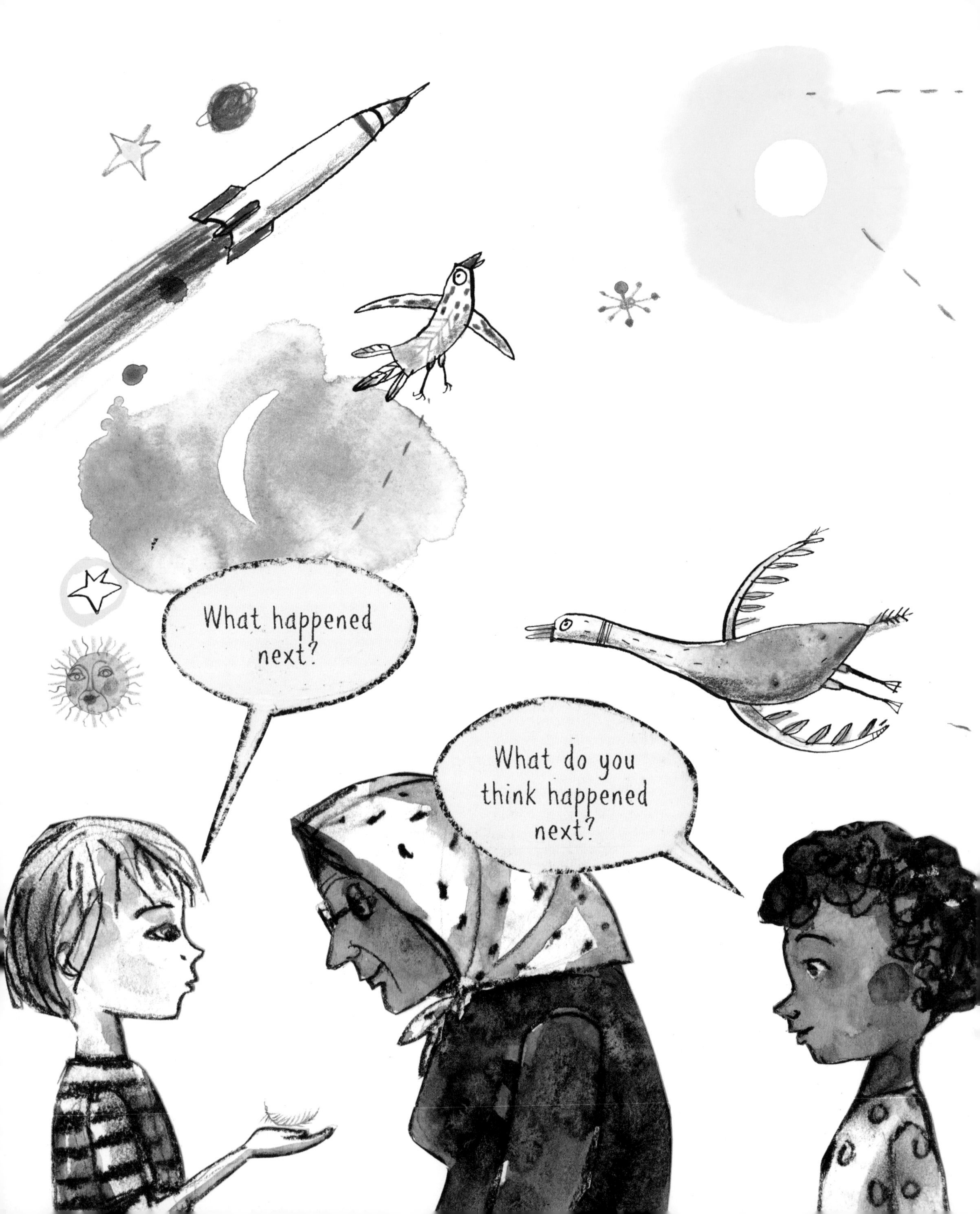
What happened next?
What do you think happened next?

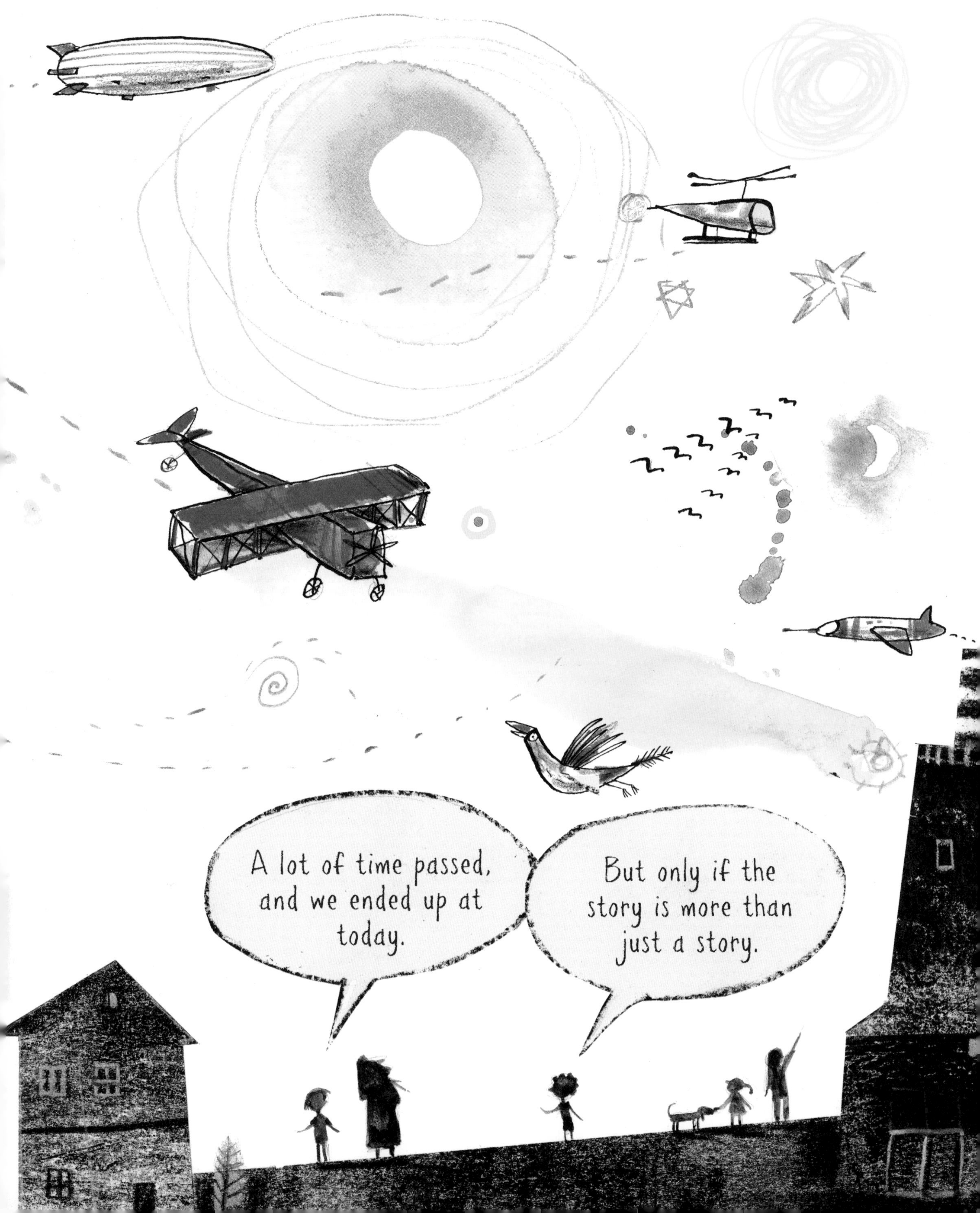
A lot of time passed, and we ended up at today.
But only if the story is more than just a story.

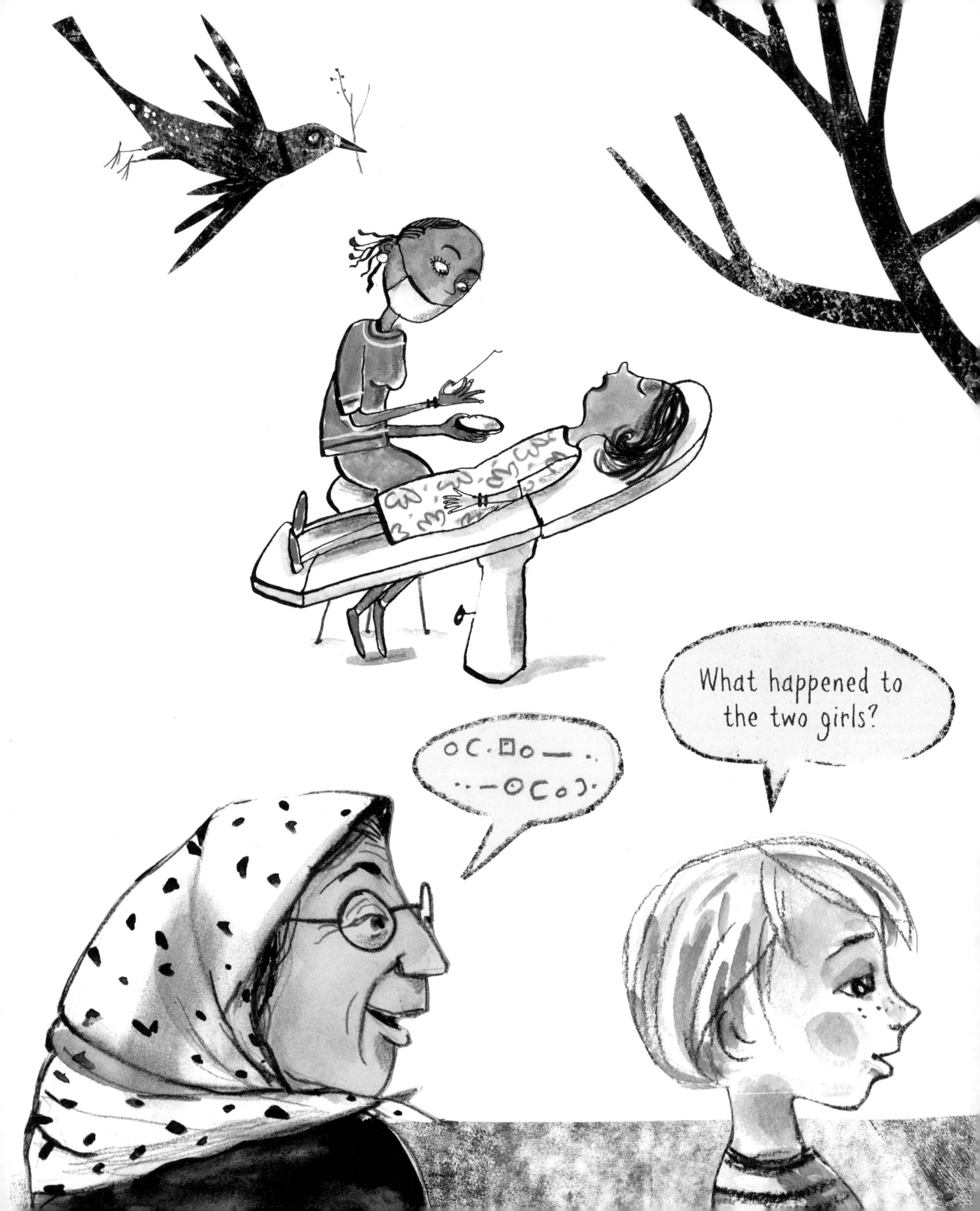
What happened to the two girls?

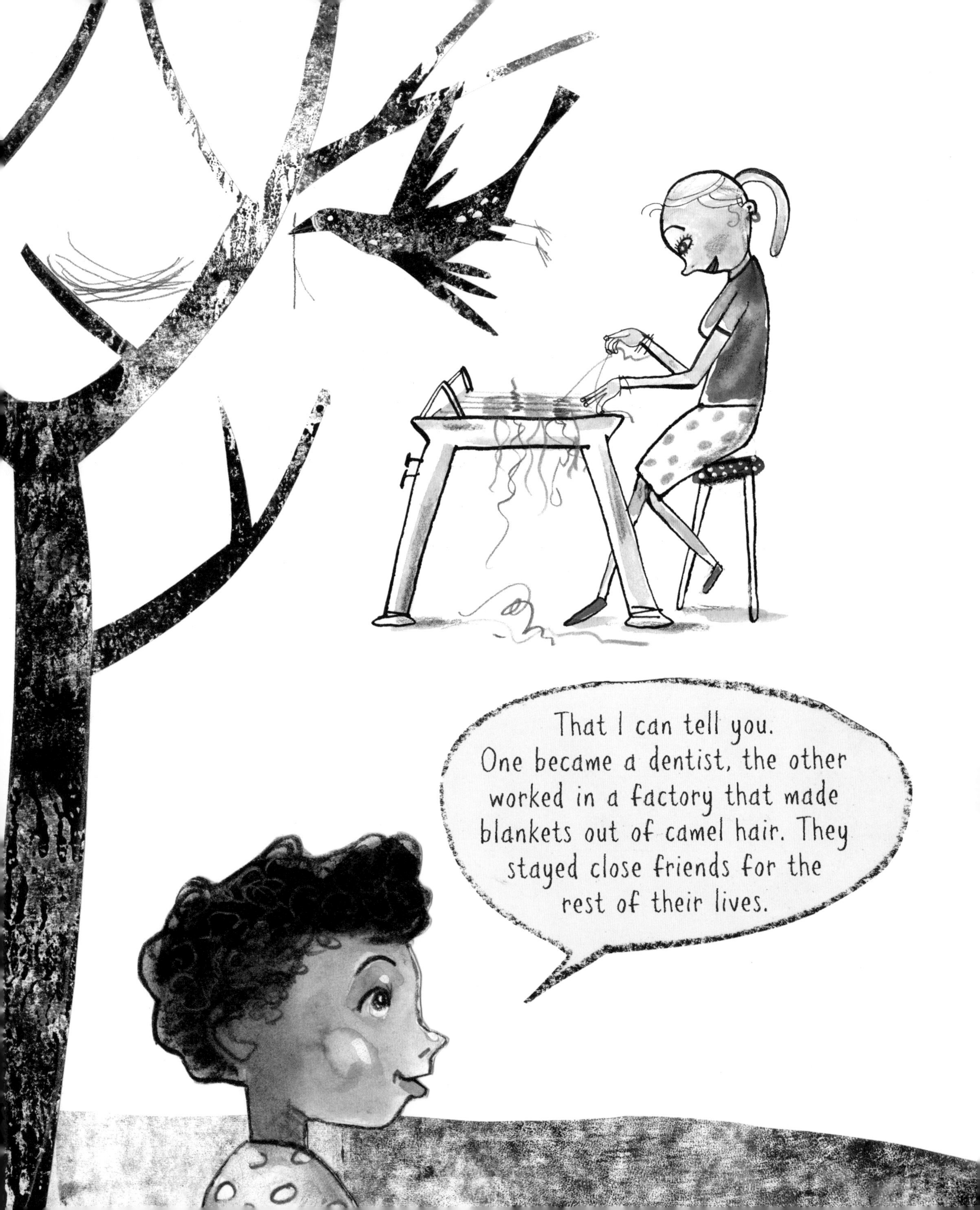
That I can tell you. One became a dentist, the other worked in a factory that made blankets out of camel hair. They stayed close friends for the rest of their lives.

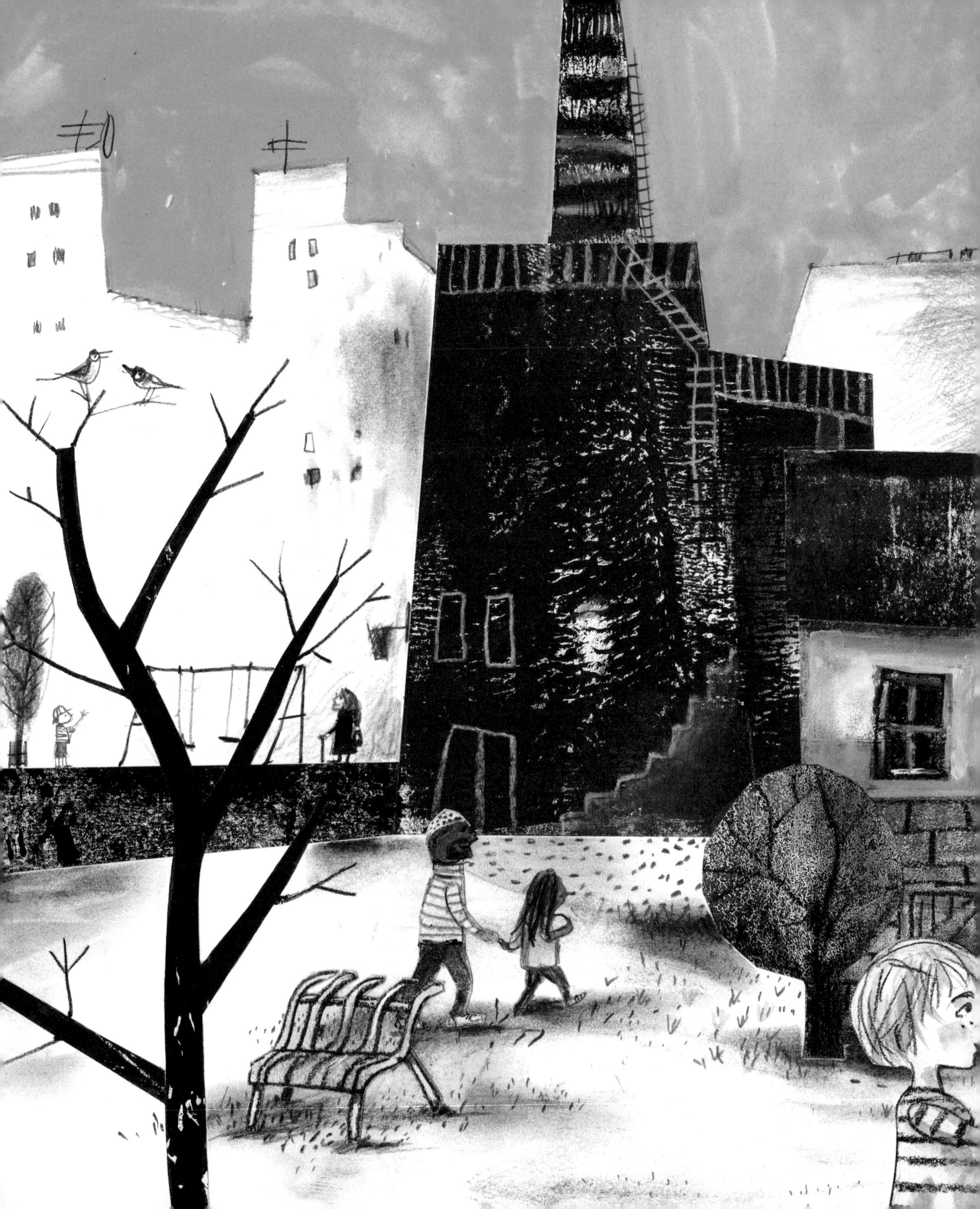

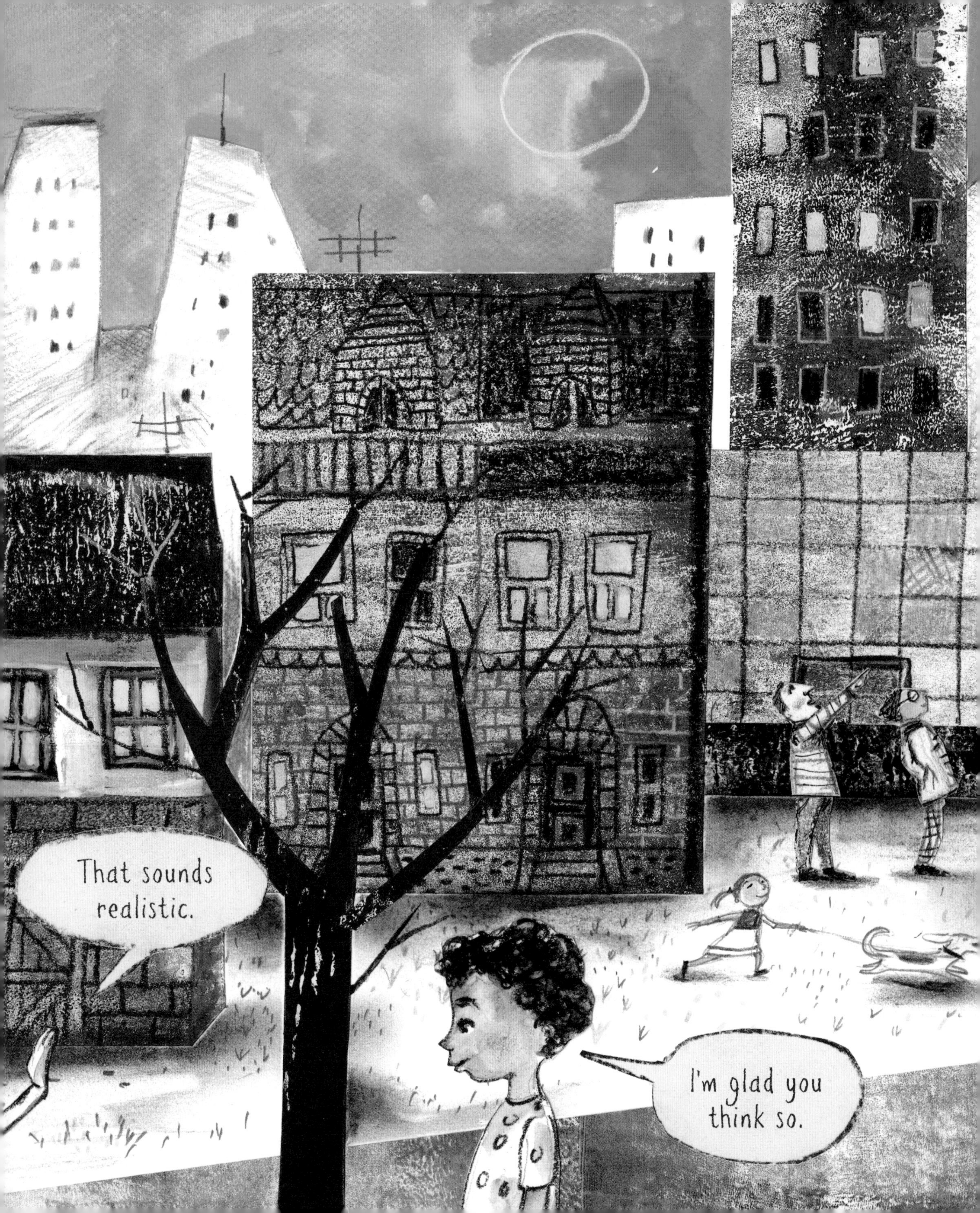
That sounds realistic.
I'm glad you think so.

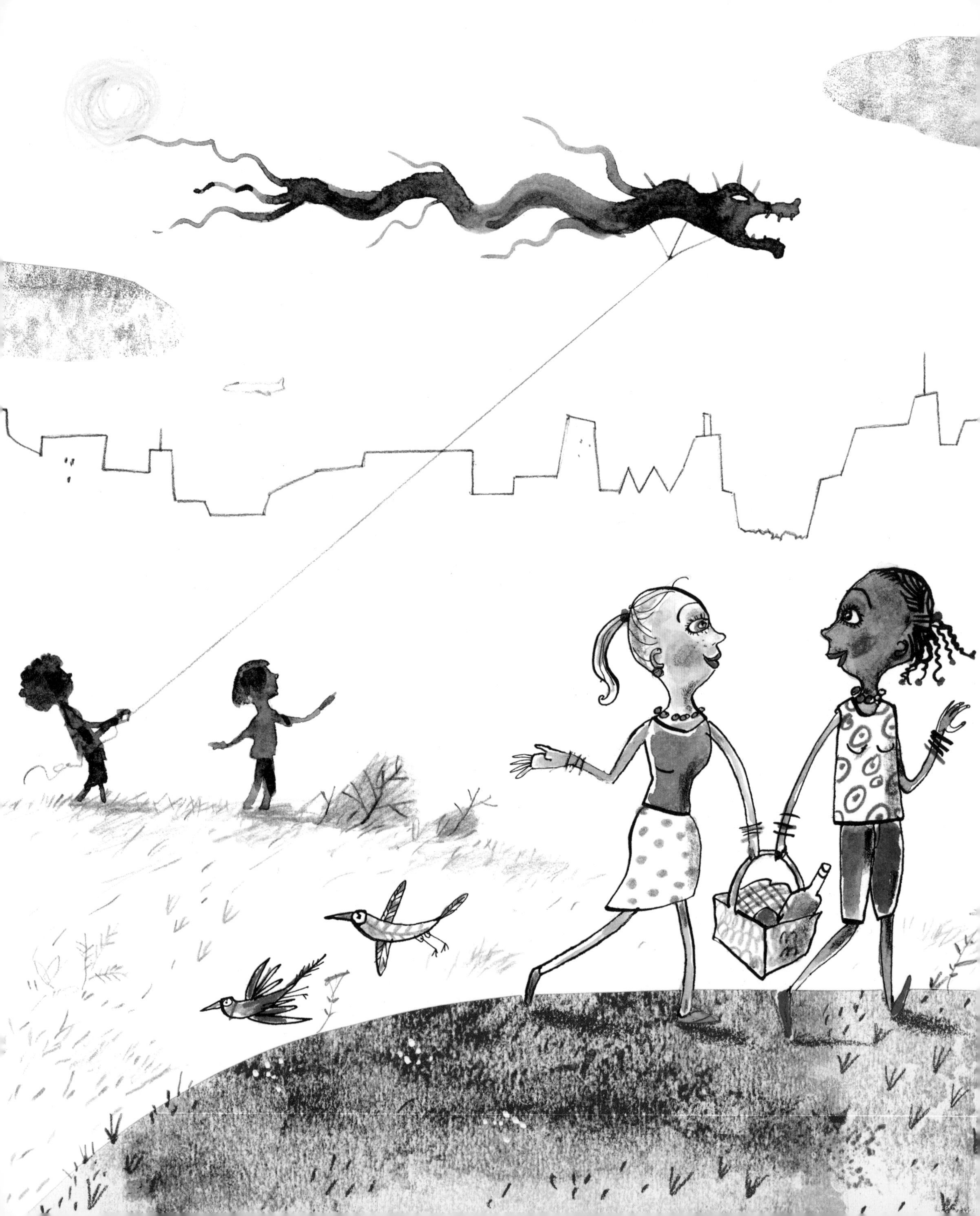

• Author's Note •

WHEN I WAS FIVE or so, my friend Michael went to Germany for six months. Not only were we friends, but our backyards were adjoining, our dads taught together, and our mothers were friends — so until his trip to Germany, we saw each other all the time.

When Michael came back from his six months away, he ran up to our back fence and called our names. My brother and I ran over to greet him — we were so excited to see him. We started asking him questions, and he answered us in German.

We said, "Michael, answer in English! You're speaking German!"

Michael looked mortified. He spoke again in German. Clearly upset, he ran back to his house.

Michael's parents were German, so while he was away, no one spoke English at all. He'd lost his conversational English in that short a period. He regained his English quickly, and when I asked him about this encounter years later, he also remembered how disconcerting it was.

When I came across the Babel story for the first time, probably at around the same age, this experience gave it a credibility it might not otherwise have had.

Many years later, when my son Ashey was little, he was fascinated by biblical stories, particularly the ones in Genesis. He liked to recount them in his own words and ask us hard-to-answer questions, such as "What happened to the imaginary animals at the time of Noah? Were they allowed to board the ark, and if not, what happened to them?" He made up dialogue for the snake in the garden of Eden and also liked to imitate God imitating the animals, which God did for fun according to Ashey.

Ashey's enthusiastic interest in (and inquisitive approach to) the Genesis stories inspired the characters of the old woman with her unfamiliar version of the Babel tale as well as the boy who repeatedly questions her. Ashey's passionate, critical and imaginative retellings of the old tales made this tale possible.

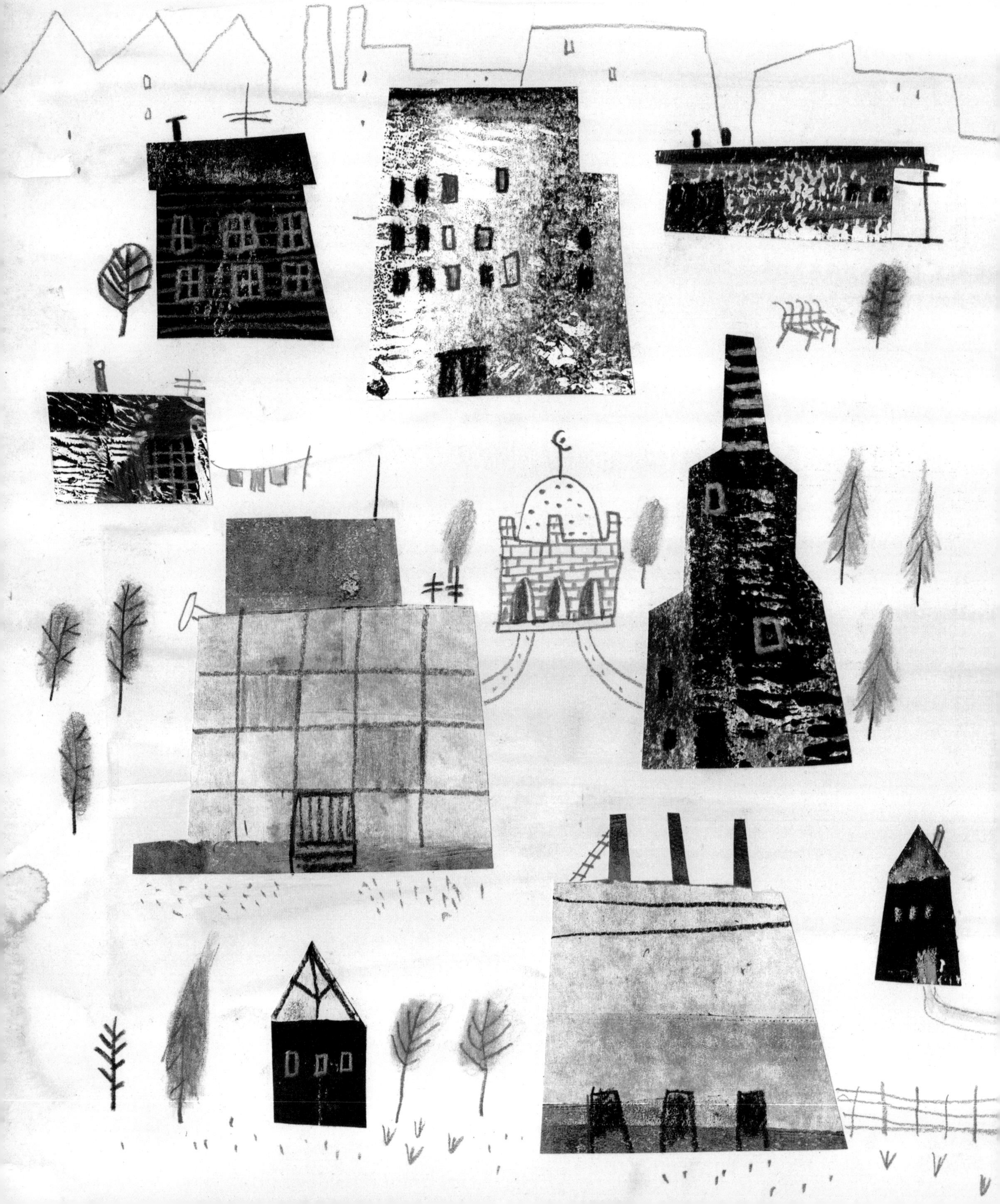